**sweet water…**
# STOLEN LAND

sweet water…
# STOLEN LAND

## Philip McLaren

Magabala Books

**sweet water...**
STOLEN LAND

New edition 2001, published by
Magabala Books Aboriginal Corporation
PO Box 668,
Broome Western Australia 6725

First Published by Queensland University Press 1993.

Also by Philip McLaren: *Scream Black Murder; Lightning Mine; There'll be New Dreams*

Magabala Books receives financial assistance from the
State Government of Western Australia through the
Department for the Arts; the Aboriginal and Torres Strait
Islander Commission; and the Aboriginal and Torres Strait
Islander Arts Board of the Australia Council, the
Federal Government's arts funding and advisory body.
The David Unaipon Award receives financial assistance
from the Queensland Office of Arts and Cultural Development.

Cover Photograph: Grahame McConnell, the Breadknife, Warrumbungle Range
Designer Narelle Jones/Jane Lodge
Printed by Frank Daniels Pty. Ltd., Western Australia
Typeset in Giovanni 11/14

National Library of Australia
Cataloguing-in-Publication data
McLaren, Philip, 1943-.
Sweet water : stolen land.
I. Title. (Series : UQP black Australian writers)
A823.3
ISBN 1 875641 77 7

Distributed in the USA and Canada by
International Specialized Book Services, Inc.,
5804 N.E. Hassalo Street, Portland, Oregon 97213-3640

# PREAMBLE

This is a novel. The settings, the characters and the majority of the incidents are fictional. There was no such place as Neuberg Mission. It is a composite of several missions of which I have personal knowledge.

Aboriginal events and stories that I have used are a mixture of existing legends and fiction. The story of the Gunnedah people is imaginary. The stories of Baiame the All-Father and the Baiame Stone Traps are actual Aboriginal legends. Most Aboriginal people written about here are also fictional.

The Myall Creek massacre did take place. Most of the events that I have described in this particular chapter did happen. I positioned my fictional Aboriginal family at the place of the horror. The massacre took place on June 9th 1838 — I took enough artistic licence to re-enact it thirty years after it actually happened. Racially motivated mass murders of Aboriginal people still occurred well into the twentieth century.

In 1947, A.O. Neville, Commissioner of Native Affairs in the state of Western Australia offered a written solution to the Aboriginal problem:

> *Scientific research had revealed that skin pigmentation could be bred out of Aborigines in two or*

*three generations. If I could only have the money and the legislative power to start a selective breeding programme I could, in a matter of sixty to seventy years, solve the 'Aboriginal problem' by breeding a race of white Aborigines.*

George Fife Angas did exist. When he personally financed German Lutheran missions his motivation appeared to be guided by Christian paternalism, but when he became active in massive land grabs his ethics were in question. His German missionaries skilfully herded Aboriginal people from their land, making its seizure and exploitation easy. The impact his missions had on Aboriginal culture is another story.

Ginny Griffin did exist; she was my great-great-grandmother. She did become leader and spokesperson for the Aboriginal people of Coonabarabran.

The town of Coonabarabran lies at the foothills of the very real, very beautiful Warrumbungle Mountains, my father's country.

*Philip McLaren*
*September, 1992*

# ONE

The raw, tumultuous outback lay open.

The horse sensed the storm ahead. His nostrils flared and he tossed his head as he sniffed the wind. There was a sudden drop in temperature — it had been a very warm day. Red dust was carried high on the wind as it swirled, gaining in velocity as it moved south across the open plains. Dark clouds rolled over the spectacular Warrumbungle Mountains towards Gudrun and Karl Maresch as they rounded a bend and headed directly into the strong wind. The rain came soon after. The wind drove the cool rain onto the faces of the newcomers. Huge icy raindrops that usually preceded hail fell in walls of water, soaking deep into the dry red loam.

Karl steered the horse and sulky off the wide stock trail to shelter behind an outcrop of sandstone boulders. He took an oilskin sheet from under the seat and pulled it over them both in a makeshift tent as they moved to sit on the floor of the buggy.

Lightning flashed all around. A mighty thunderclap directly overhead caused Gudrun to tense her grip on Karl's arm. He was of true stoic German character.

He knew Gudrun feared electrical storms yet he could not find it in himself to comfort her.

They had been to Gunnedah. It was an unusual trip for them to make because the Coonabarabran township was much closer. But Karl had decided they should see Gunnedah in the summer. It was 1869, an exciting time in Australia. The newly settled land declared its challenge to the adventurous.

Coonabarabran, along with almost every plains community in Australia, had already planned its future based on agriculture: wool, wheat and cash crops for the tables of Europe. A certain Lewis Gordon first proposed a town plan survey for Coonabarabran in 1859 although the area had been opened up by a Government sponsored expedition in 1817.

"The storm's moving quickly," Karl said quietly in German. "It will blow over soon." He was wrong; the lightning became more frequent, the rain heavier.

Gudrun was often bemused by the fact that she now lived in Australia. She had never seriously considered living abroad, although when she was in her early teens occasionally she thought it might be exciting to live in London for a time — she spoke English very well. Then she met Karl Maresch and was totally swept off her feet. He was so confident. He had strong, unwavering opinions about the world that he couched in well developed philosophical and theological argument. To a young woman growing up on a farm on the outskirts of Munich, he was every inch the intellectual. He had read the lesson frequently at her church and took charge of a Bible class that she attended during the week. She had always admired him, even when she was a little girl. Gudrun was nineteen and Karl thirty-five when they married four years ago. The simple ceremony was conducted by his father, also a Lutheran pastor, in the tiny church at Grafing, south of Munich.

Lightning flashed and thunder followed immediately. Now the storm's centre was directly overhead. In another bright flash Gudrun suddenly saw an Aboriginal family sitting opposite them. They were huddled together, sheltering under an overhanging rock about thirty yards away across a small clearing.

The Aboriginal family — a man, his wife and two children — were looking at the white-skinned Europeans under their makeshift shelter on the horse buggy.

Ginny and Wollumbuy were married under Aboriginal law. Both their families still followed the old ways. At first it was said they could not marry, but later a way was found so that they could conform to complicated kinship laws. Wollumbuy first saw Ginny when he came to visit her clan several summers ago at Gunnedah, where she was born and raised. His own large family had walked more than one hundred and fifty miles over the mountains from their camp on the coast near the newly-built town of Coffs Harbour. It was a very long walk of the kind families used to make. Wollumbuy sang Ginny his love songs and she heard them in her sleep. He danced a magic, erotic love dance for her around the campfire and she awoke feeling stirred and excited. Their two children came quickly, answering the hope and tradition of Kamilaroi marriages.

Now Ginny took her youngest to her breast. He needed comfort from the storm.

The wind blew in on them and Wollumbuy grimaced as another thunderclap shattered the air. He grabbed at the stone talisman Ginny's mother had made for him as a wedding gift which he always had hanging from his belt. He held it firmly.

They had come from Gunnedah to set up camp at the foot of Old Belougerie, a massive sacred rock spire that rose vertically from the foot of the mountains, towering high above the well-treed peaks. His people knew that the good spirits protected all people living within sight of the rock so that they lived long and happy lives.

Ginny suspected that some day Wollumbuy would want to take her back to his father's country, to stay at his home at Moonee beach camp. She thought it would be exciting to live near Belougerie, even for a short while. Large Aboriginal camps were seen less now than ever before. The Kamilaroi people had been forced off their ancestral lands onto hastily established missions. The whites were building fences everywhere. They had no regard for wild life, no understanding or feeling for the land. All hunting would soon be ruined. They had already cleared far too many plants and trees. Her three favourite bunyah-bunyah nut trees were destroyed last year to make way for more grazing land for sheep and other animals whose cloven hooves destroyed the delicate topsoil and laid bare the earth.

White people actually wanted to own the land! She wondered secretly if some day they would claim ownership of the sky, the stars, the clouds, the rain, the rivers and the ocean. She suspected that if they could find a way to do it, they would.

"There, I think it's stopped," Karl said, almost in a whisper. The rain had eased but it certainly had not stopped. As he pulled the oilskin back, small pools of water that had collected on it ran down his arms under the sleeves of his jacket. He cursed, wiped the water away and took up the reins. He called to the horse as he sat upright on the leather upholstered seat. They were on their way again. The Neuberg Lutheran mission was only a couple of hours away. It was thirty miles from Coonabarabran and fifty-five miles from Gunnedah, built at the foot of Baraba Mountain on the eastern side of the Warrumbungle Range. Lutherans made ideal missionaries. They were well received by almost all international governments because of their basic belief that the State ought to be above the church.

Ninety years ago, Australia was built by convict labour. The government of Mother England transported convicts to aid the colonisation of the large South Land. The number of convicts needed for the planned settlements seemed to override more important criteria for transportation, such as skills, age or marital status. Fleets of convict slaves sailed south. The wretched human cargo knew little about the colonies, except for terrifying rumours of black savages and strange animals that aided Satan's work in a new-fashioned hell.

The Australian Government was still benefiting from the gold rush of the previous decade, which brought with it a huge influx of free immigrants. Whole towns sprang up overnight as the plains west of Sydney offered up their riches. Now plans of bigger proportions were being hatched; anything seemed possible. But the problem that always caused delay was the scarcity of labour. Back in England, the idea that transportation was a beneficial and morally sound way to rehabilitate prisoners had nowadays to be demonstrated to the government.

The colony of South Australia was founded in 1834 by free settlers. They were wealthy Nonconformists dissatisfied with government rule in England; they banded together to form the South Australian Colonisation Committee. One of its members, George Fife Angas, emigrated to South Australia in 1848. He put forward his high-flown reasons for a new settlement:

> *My great object was in the first instance to provide a place of refuge for pious Dissenters of Great Britain who could in their new home discharge their consciences before God in civil and religious duties without any disabilities. Then to provide a place where the children of pious farmers might have farms in which to settle and provide bread for their families; and lastly that I may be the humble instrument of laying the foundation of a good system of education and religious instruction for the poorer settlers.*

Angas advanced the princely sum of eight thousand pounds to entice persecuted Prussian Lutherans into establishing missions to *enable Aborigines to come to where they might worship God and at the same time bind them to the missions as tenant farmers for a mandatory thirty years*. As well as destroying large segments of

Aboriginal culture for ever, Angas had put in place his perfectly legal method of solving the rising costs of labour: the enslavement of Australia's Aboriginal people. Yet slavery was something he had publicly opposed forty years earlier in England. Obviously, when it came to his private business dealings a different set of principles applied.

Filled with righteousness and armed with faith, the Lutherans ventured to outback Australia to convert the Aboriginal people — to tell them, with absolute conviction, that forty thousand years of Aboriginal Dreaming was wrong. They passed on the word of the Lord and set about redeeming the heathen Australians through education, Christian principles and ethics, and tenant farming.

When the letter of offer came for Karl to take up an Australian mission, he positively swelled with pride. Now he was Pastor Maresch of Neuberg Mission, saviour of souls.

Through the rainy haze, on a distant knoll, Gudrun again saw the small Aboriginal family walking along the muddy trail ahead of them. "We should offer them a ride," she insisted, "Look at them, they're soaked!"

Rain was still falling heavily as they drew alongside the family. Wollumbuy moved to the side of the trail to allow the buggy to pass. Ginny looked up at Gudrun with a question written on her face. She was carrying her baby; her two-year-old boy walked with his father.

"Yes, come on," Gudrun said as she leaned down and stretched out her arm to help the young mother onto the buggy.

Karl said nothing. Gudrun knew he didn't approve. She acted with haste so as to give him little room for refusal. He brought the buggy, already heavily laden, to a stop. All four climbed on the back, and Gudrun gave a wide friendly smile as she spread the oilskin over their heads. They continued on their way through the drenching rain.

"Thank you," Ginny said. Gudrun squeezed Karl's arm. Nothing more was said for the remaining hour and a half as the old grey horse pulled its heavy load along the muddy road to Neuberg Mission.

The Mission, named after a Bavarian village in which Karl grew up was methodical in its layout. Pastor Maresch had spent two weeks with town planners and an architect in Sydney before actually seeing the site of his mission. He worked from the basic land survey plan. He had to include so many things he just hadn't considered. Basic things such as waste: night soil and garbage must be disposed of in a hygienic manner. He had to plan adequate water supply for the population, which he expected would reach around two hundred. Stores and provisions must be considered as well as law and order. A cemetery, a school and a church were included in the plans. Karl allocated the high ground at the foothills of Baraba Mountain to himself as the site for the house he would build Gudrun. It would be made from timber, with plenty of windows, a large porch and would overlook the whole valley. He had promised Gudrun's parents that he would provide her with a good home.

Gudrun's parents were Prussians. They came south to Bavaria after Napoleon overran the new German state at Jena. Gudrun, their only child, received the undivided love of both parents, to whom she was totally devoted. She never felt deprived of anything. Her parents managed well enough off the land but they had little money left over. They insisted she go with them whenever they took their farm produce to market in Munich. The horse-drawn cart would be overflowing with sacks and wooden crates for the journey, and Gudrun used to sit on top. On colder days she would settle down into the vegetables, out of the wind.

While her parents were busy selling at their market stall, Gudrun would stroll to the Marien Platz. Here she could dream. The collection of shops in this huge square was unequalled anywhere in Prussia. Gudrun would press her nose against the shop windows with their wonderful displays of shoes from Italy, clothes from Paris, exotic breads, pastries and cakes, furniture, fine art … and she would dream. She would always stay long enough to experience the magic moments every hour when the Marien Platz clock came to life. It was a fine example of the craftsmanship of master clocksmiths of the period: to the entranced little girl standing in the square it was pure magic. Every hour it would open its doors and a cast of beautifully carved and painted characters paraded onto its stage. Twisting and turning, nodding and bowing, they made a clockwork carousel that held visitors and townspeople alike spellbound.

The buggy slipped dangerously sideways off the trail as Karl steered for the gates of the mission. Wollumbuy was quick to act. He jumped from the cart, pushing against the buggy wheel to prevent it colliding with the posts as the horse, reined in by Karl, pulled the cart past the gate. Karl didn't bring the buggy to a stop until he was well inside the mission grounds. Then he turned to speak to Wollumbuy. "You and your family are welcome to stay on our mission," he said.

"It is a good place for you to raise your children," Gudrun added quickly.

Ginny looked at Wollumbuy.

"No, thanks. We're going to Belougerie," Wollumbuy replied. Shyly he diverted his eyes to the ground.

"How far away is that?" Karl asked.

"It's down past Coonabarabran town, past Timor Rock, along the river."

"Can you come to church here sometimes?" Karl went on, forcing the issue. "Your people all like it here, we help them. We are teachers. It's not all church and God here like the other places."

Gudrun had heard Karl use this tired form of persuasion so often she could almost scream.

"No, thanks. We'll be all right." Wollumbuy turned to help Ginny and the children down from the buggy.

"Thank you," Ginny said softly to Gudrun. Gudrun nodded and pursed her lips in a crooked half-smile.

Then Ginny, Wollumbuy and the children walked back onto the trail and continued on their way. Their scanty clothing was drenched through. The young boy was enjoying walking with his father in the deep mud. Ginny carried her baby and walked behind. When she reached the gate, she looked back.

Gudrun called to her. "What's your name?" She thought she heard the Aboriginal woman answer "Jildi" — or was it "Ginny"? Gudrun smiled again and waved. She hoped Ginny would talk her man into coming to live at the mission. It needed more young couples with children if it was to succeed.

# TWO

Ginny was ten years old when a school teacher named Winifred Jackson moved into the abandoned squatter's cottage near the small creek on the outskirts of Gunnedah. Winifred was fifty-two, a well-groomed lady from Manchester. She had no husband and no children of her own.

She first saw Ginny wading in the shallows of the creek. "Be careful, those rocks can be slippery!" she called to her. At that time Ginny had heard very little English, and so she had no idea what the tall lady was saying. Her reply, a big smile, totally disarmed the teacher. She beckoned Ginny to join her. For an instant Ginny hesitated, then quickly jumped and skipped her way down the steep slope.

"Do you live around here?" Winifred asked.

"Around … here." Ginny imitated the sounds, wanting desperately to communicate. She exaggerated the shapes the English woman made with her mouth as she formed her words.

"Yes, but where?" Winifred asked.

"But … where," Ginny mimicked.

"Oh … I see, we have a parrot here, do we?"

Winifred smiled, reached into her deep apron pocket and pulled out a spoon.

"Do ... we," Ginny said. She was pleased that she could say some of the strange words.

"Spoon," Winifred said, pointing to the object in her left hand.

Ginny's face brightened as she realised the white lady's intention. "Spoon," she said smugly.

"Again ... spoon."

"Spoon."

"Good." Winifred looked toward a nearby gum tree. "Tree," she said.

"Tree," said the parrot.

"That's right, tree."

"That's right, tree," the parrot echoed.

Winifred stifled a laugh. "Grass," she said, pointing to the ground.

"Grass."

Winifred held the spoon high, raised her eyebrows and nodded her head, asking a question.

The parrot understood. "Spoon," she replied.

They both laughed loudly as they realised Ginny was beginning to understand. Such was Ginny's formal introduction to the English language.

Every afternoon, Winifred's smile quickened at the sight of the Aboriginal girl waiting beside the waterfall near the house. They had become unlikely friends. Ginny realised she was lucky that her new neighbour taught children to read and write. When the women of her tribe arrived back from their gathering each day, Ginny walked from her camp across two fenced fields, through the forest of tall gum trees behind Winifred's house and waited for her to come home. While Ginny watched and waited she would sing the songs Winifred had taught her.

"All the King's horses and all the King's men couldn't put Humpty together again," she sang sweetly.

# THREE

Winter passed quickly at Neuberg mission. Now it was stifling hot and humid; Gudrun's thoughts were of Christmas. She had asked Karl some time ago to allow her to organise a choir. She knew that if she worked hard they could be ready to sing at the Christmas service. But Karl was reluctant to relinquish any part of his empire.

Gudrun was sitting on the porch sewing a dress when she noticed red dust on the horizon. "Someone's coming ... on horseback," she called to Karl through the open door. He was lying on the couch with his feet on the armrest, reading. He didn't answer Gudrun immediately, preferring to continue with his book.

"Who do you think it is?" he said finally.

Visitors on horseback were usually Europeans. There had been no European visitor for eight months. Gudrun felt a surge of anxiety in the pit of her stomach. She finished off her sewing to a stage where she could leave it and bundled it neatly into her basket. Then she stood up, straining her eyes at the dust in the distance, shielding them from the hot sun with her fan. "They are coming on the Tambar Springs trail," she said slowly.

Karl stopped reading his book and walked onto the porch next to his wife. He didn't say anything. Nervously Gudrun began to gather odd items and walked inside. She emerged with a broom fashioned from ti-tree and started to sweep the floor. She noticed some stray garbage on the grassy area in front of the house and ran down to retrieve it. She looked again at the dust raised by the travellers when she returned to the steps.

"They should be here in about an hour. I suppose I'd better get washed and shaved," Karl said.

"That would be nice," Gudrun said with a smile. She would never mention it but Karl hadn't been shaving as often as he used to. Sometimes he sported whiskers for a week. She continued sweeping. When she had finished the floor she swept away some spider webs from under the porch roof. She glanced through the open front door and smiled to herself when she heard Karl singing and splashing at his wash-basin.

Almost exactly an hour later Gudrun walked onto the porch and sat in her chair. Not far in the distance, in breaks between trees, she could see two men on horses. They rode at a slow walking pace, one in front of the other.

"They'll be here in a minute!" she called to Karl.

Karl didn't really like visitors. When he was a boy and relatives came to visit his family, he recalled how he used to hide. His father, as a Lutheran pastor, always had people calling at their home. There was a certain level of social contact that was tolerable for Karl after which he would switch off. He preferred to be alone and enjoyed his own company. He would fantasise about what he would do to change the world.

Karl had particularly hated Mrs Hosendoffer's visits at his boyhood home. She always smelled of orange-scented talcum powder. He thought she wore too much face powder, it made her look as if she was dead. Her husband had long since died. Mrs Hosendoffer would insist on kissing Karl twice, once on each cheek. Then she would hug him, pull him to her, hold him tightly against her huge breasts and not release him until she felt him struggling for freedom. When she left she would kiss him on the mouth, rubbing her wet lips against his. In fact, Mrs Hosendoffer had been an alcoholic, though of course he did not know that.

Karl remembered the time he stayed with the Hosendoffer family for a holiday weekend. She had him cornered, at her mercy. Mrs Hosendoffer lived with her three giggling daughters but she chose Karl to torment with her distorted affection. She walked in on him when he was taking a bath and insisted on washing him. Bathing him in a furious lather of soap, she never once diverted her eyes from his penis. Finally, exhausted, she made him get out of the bath while she dried him until his skin was sore.

"I always wanted a boy," she told him, rubbing him with a towel with rasp-like fibres.

The mission dogs had picked up the scent of the visitors and began their chorus. Some of the younger pups started to move towards the gates to voice their welcome. A few Aboriginal people came out of their huts to see what the commotion was all about. Their children ran with the dogs to the gate. Karl came out onto the porch and sat next to his wife.

Most of the Aboriginal mission population were home for the weekend. Those who chose to work were back from the sheep stations or building sites in town. Some worked six days a week, resting on Sundays on the remote stations; they did not return for weeks at a time. The remainder had not decided if the European money system was for them. Some of the men still hunted and the women gathered in much the same way as the Kamilaroi people had done in this region for centuries. When European-style traps were introduced it made the men's lot easier, but traditional life for the women remained physically hard. It was mostly the women who chose to live on the mission. It meant relief from that harsh traditional role.

The two horsemen, an Aborigine and a bearded European, had finally reached the gate. Each carried a large pack on his horse. The children ran up to the men as they dismounted. There was great excitement; the white man took off his hat and dusted his clothes down, looking about and laughing with the children as they tugged at his clothes. The mission dogs yapped and jumped in frenzied delight. Then he glanced up towards the house on the hill where Gudrun and Karl stood looking down. He waved to them, good-natured-ly brushed the children aside and made his way up the rise. His Aboriginal companion walked with him, smiling and speaking in his native tongue to the children.

Karl walked down the steps from the porch to greet the men. "Good morning, I am Karl Maresch."

He extended his hand very deliberately. He was dressed in the dark trousers, shirt and tie normally held in reserve for church. His long, dark hair, now half-grey, was swept back and tied. He wore his sideburns long and well-trimmed. Karl had made an effort to create a good impression.

"How do you do. I am Douglas Langton," the tall stranger responded in a cultured English accent.

Karl turned and in a wide gesture introduced Gudrun. "This is my wife."

Gudrun felt Douglas Langton's light blue eyes penetrate hers as he directed his gaze towards her. She was embarrassed to feel a flush flood her cheeks. No one had looked at her like that for many years.

Suddenly she recalled her adolescent sweetheart, Helmar Scholtz. Helmar's eyes were also light blue. She had allowed him to kiss her on the way home from school so that she could look deep into his eyes. He kissed her for other reasons. He carried her books and followed her every wish. When he looked into her eyes she was lost.

Gudrun liked the way Douglas looked at her now. She wore an ankle-length light green dress, trimmed with lace at the neck and sleeves. She had perfect skin, and the tips of her ears, cheeks and nose glowed pinkly. She had a large, well defined bosom that pressed its shape forward through her dress. Her long blonde hair was pinned up on her head.

"How do you do," Douglas Langton said. He took her hand and kissed it softly. It was a manner of greeting he had learned to use in France.

Gudrun pulled her hand away quickly, still blushing. She felt a tingling sensation as his soft, moist lips lingered on her skin.

Karl noticed that his wife seemed uncomfortable. "Please, come and sit down and take some tea with us," he said, walking back up the steps. Gudrun smiled and stole a glance of the stranger before going inside to prepare the tea.

Douglas watched the sway of Gudrun's hips as she scurried away. Her bare ankles were just visible beneath the hem of her long dress.

Wollumbuy bent low to stay out of sight of the grazing kangaroos. He moved slowly, placing his spears and boomerangs at his feet except for one very long spear which he fixed to his woomera. Then, in an explosion of energy he sprang to his full height and ran and skipped sideways as he put his whole body weight behind a mighty thrust of his hunting spear. The javelin quivered from the initial thrust then the spear-head broke the air and rode on it. It struck its prey high in the chest: the kangaroo fell heavily and awkwardly in the high grass. Wollumbuy sprinted to the kangaroo and began his apologies and thanks to the animal according to the custom of the Kamilaroi hunter when he took the life of his prey. He released his spear and prepared the animal for carrying. It was a short walk back to his camp at Belougerie.

From their Gunyah, Ginny saw Wollumbuy across the grassy plains and yelped her delight when she realised he was carrying a kangaroo on his head. They had made their camp near others at the foot of the huge rock spire. Their single shelter consisted of sheets of bark skilfully taken from a tree and applied to branches selected for their elasticity. The result was a large shack with a curved roof. All daily life was conducted outdoors unless it was too hot or someone was ill. The gunyah was for sleeping and sheltering from rain. It was constructed conveniently near a shade tree that Ginny and Wollumbuy quickly adopted and claimed as family. They took care of the tree and spoke to it often. Their campfire was between the tree and the gunyah. A stream ran close by, providing ample water and doubling as a refreshing swimming-hole during the hot summer months.

The children and Ginny ran across the plains to greet Wollumbuy, who was wearing a big proud grin. When he reached the camp he built and lit the fire, and together with Ginny prepared the kangaroo for baking in the coals. They chose the parts they wanted for themselves; the remainder they would distribute among their many neighbours, as custom decreed.

That night a large group settled around Wollumbuy's fire after their feast of kangaroo. Ginny was asked once again to tell how her ancestors came to Gunnedah. Taking her youngest to her breast, she began the story of Lorita and Wahbuk, the ancestors who founded her clan...

*The story of the Gunnedah people:*

*On an east coast beach of the great land the sky took on a strange colour for the second consecutive day. The day before it had been orange; today it glowed red.*

Lorita, the youngest of the ceremonial chief's daughters, was already on the beach looking at the strange red sky. Someone called to her; she hurried back to the camp to join the others.

The gathering of the women of the tribe, as always, took place early. The children ran and played and cried. The women sat and discussed where they would fossick, dig, and gather the day's food.

The men, worried about the weather, were already considering moving the camp to the protection offered by the inland caves. All was not right with their world. The ocean pushed continually at the sandy beach; an unseen downward pressure had forced the sea flat. A wave broke free occasionally to run higher onto the sand. The red sky was mirrored in the warm, light-green water.

Suddenly, a dark cloud appeared on the horizon, driven by a strong wind towards the coast. The red sky was being overwhelmed by the grey cloud. The people began to get nervous. The women hurried back to camp, the younger ones carrying the nuts and berries they had begun to gather. The men were chattering excitedly when they arrived. The dark cloud swept over the camp and a torrential downpour fell from it. The heavy rain was driven by a strong wind that blew with a fury never before experienced.

The people fled in an organised pattern, following the old men who led them along a path to the inland and shelter. The trees waved and flexed in a demented dance. The Kamilaroi people watched as their traditional paths were blocked by large, uprooted trees. Lightning flashed and thunder crashed all around the fleeing group. Lorita contained her fear as best she could.

Two older men, anticipating the worst, decided they should head for a big coastal cave instead of following the original plan to go to the larger, well established havens farther away. The cave had a small opening, making it difficult to find. The long, deep hollow guaranteed shelter. Paintings decorated the ceiling and walls. The Kamilaroi had used this cave for thousands of years. Firewood was always stocked here for emergencies. Usually the emergency was a raiding party from a nearby tribe, young men looking for women. This was different: someone had really angered the spirits. Their Kamilaroi ancestors were making it known they were not happy.

A group of younger men bravely volunteered to go back and guide the rest of tribe to the safety of the huge sandstone hollows.

In case this strange phenomena should reoccur, the Kamilaroi people decided to expand their clan further inland. Their numbers were becoming large and it was difficult to remember everyone's names. An extension clan of fifty, twenty-five couples, would be selected from the young. A prerequisite for being chosen was the possession of a skill such as food gathering, spear-making, hunting, fishing, weaving, magic, medicine, storytelling, singing or dancing...

Although she was sad to leave her family, Lorita was excited when she was chosen to go. Her parents were proud of their daughter. She would be helping to found a new branch of Kamilaroi people. Lorita was very good at gathering fruits, nuts and berries and she was well schooled in medicine by her father.

Marriages were hurriedly organised followed by departing celebrations that took several weeks to prepare *and complete. Lorita was married to Wahbuk; he sang his magic love song for her and she heard him in her sleep. He was tall, a hunter and a good runner, therefore he was also a message carrier.*

*Lorita and Wahbuk and the larger part of the extension group finally settled at the foot of the Warrumbungle Mountain range. The group had decided to split up. Eventually they made three permanent river camps during the long journey. One camp was at Murrurundi, another at Quirindi and the last at Gunnedah.*

*This branch of the Kamilaroi people now stretched a very long way inland. In time, the language became spoken farther inland still because of increased trading with other clans over the many generations since the day of the red sky. The dialect became distorted and a good ear was needed to understand the original tongue. Travel stones were compulsory if anyone wanted to reach the coast. These had to be engraved by a tribesman with knowledge of secret travel markings. No uninitiated men and certainly no women were allowed to handle those magic stones...*

*So it was that Lorita and Wahbuk began Ginny's branch of the Kamilaroi, the Gunnedah clan, some 15,000 years before the birth of Christ.*

*They knew nothing of the scientific supposition that a massive meteor plummeted into the South Pacific Ocean about 17,000 years ago, plunging the earth into a greenhouse effect from which it took centuries to recover. The ice which covered large land masses of the world began to retreat rapidly to the poles, bringing earth's most recent ice age near its end. Global warming improved living conditions in coastal Australia.*

As Ginny came to the end of the story, she told how the coastal Kamilaroi people of the great southern land still enjoy the warm current that brings fish to their waters. They tell of the dolphins who inherit the spirit of dead Kamilaroi elders and herd fish towards the pronged spears of hunters waiting on the beaches.

The children fell asleep quickly after the story-telling and the neighbours left Ginny and Wollumbuy's camp. The campfire embers were still glowing in the darkness, a reminder of the meal consumed.

Wollumbuy and Ginny quietly moved to recline under their shade tree. Slowly Wollumbuy's hands began to caress Ginny's young nubile body. Soon they were naked. Ginny gave a long, high pitched moan of approval as Wollumbuy rolled on top of her. Soon they were both consumed by pent-up passion which blocked out all memory of a perfect day.

# FOUR

"What brings you to Neuberg Mission, Mr Langton?" Karl asked deliberately, after the unexpected visitor was seated on the porch.

"I'm a painter. I've heard about your Warrumbungle Mountains and I wanted to see them for myself. They might provide enough interest for a whole exhibition of paintings."

"I'm sure they would. They are marvellous. If you'd gone over the next rise you would have seen them in the distance." Karl became more relaxed as he took control of the conversation. "They stretch for about a hundred miles ... they reach their peak about forty miles from here. I'll walk you to the top of the rise later and you will see. Have you travelled far?"

"We've come from Sydney. We've been on the road for ten days — today we've probably travelled about thirty miles," Douglas said.

Gudrun reappeared at the door. She stood there listening to the two men talk. Stealing the odd glance at the stranger.

"It's really dusty out here. Do you get much rain?" Douglas asked.

"A lot. Semi-tropical flash storms. We seldom get drizzling rain. The falls are good but the problem is that it runs away from us, down an elaborate tributary system that eventually become major rivers. Farther downstream the pastures are more lush and fertile than you see around here." Karl noticed Douglas glance beyond him. He turned his head and saw Gudrun at the door. "Come, join us, dear. Mr Langton is an artist. He is here to paint the Warrumbungles."

After several cups of tea and a lot of small talk Douglas noticed his Aboriginal companion sitting on the grass near the steps. He held the horses on a long rein as they grazed.

"Let me introduce my guide and good friend. — Mar-weel! Come up here."

Mar-weel let go of the horses' reins. He smiled as he walked up the steps to the group. He was a tall, dark-skinned man with long, loose, curly hair. His large teeth protruded when he smiled. He wore riding boots, loose fitting heavy trousers, a long-sleeved shirt with the sleeves rolled up above the elbows and a wide, flat-brimmed hat.

"Mar-weel, meet Pastor and Mrs Maresch," Douglas said cheerfully.

Karl jumped to his feet and walked forward to shake Mar-weel's hand. Gudrun smiled.

"Good day, how are you?" Mar-weel said in a quiet throaty voice.

"Would you like some tea, Mar-weel?" Gudrun asked.

"Me? … No, thanks … I don't like tea too much," he answered quickly.

"Mar-weel likes his beer," Douglas said with a smile.

"We don't allow liquor on the mission," Karl said firmly.

"Oh, I'm sorry." Douglas seemed embarrassed.

"You weren't to know," Gudrun told him. She stood up, pleased to be animated, collected the cups and went inside the house.

Mar-weel was uncomfortable on the porch. He shuffled from one foot to the other, looked away across the valley and offered an excuse to leave. "One of the fellas down there knows my brother. He wants me to go and see him." Slowly he backed away.

"That's all right, Mar-weel, I'll see you shortly. Where is this fellow's place?"

"It's that fella over there, near the big tree." Mar-weel pointed to an Aboriginal man sitting in front of one of a number of huts — there looked to be about four or five geometrically grouped into five areas. They were connected by a straight red dirt road. The freshly painted white church was at the end of the road, the mission school next to it. Behind the school was the burial ground.

Douglas sensed that while the mission looked a friendly inviting place it was probably firmly run by its Pastor. "Mar-weel's an excellent guide," he told Karl.

"They make good guides all right, the Abos," Karl responded. "It's a sort of pride in their bushmanship. It's a family endorsement, that their father's taught them well."

Gudrun appeared again. She stood beside Douglas looking out over the mission. She was very conscious of standing so close to the stranger. She could smell his musky male odour.

Douglas glanced at her hands. She had long fingers with short, well-kept nails. She wore one ring, a gold wedding band. He stirred and shuffled, slightly confused, and brought his thoughts back to the situation at hand. "Where would be a good place to make camp?"

Gudrun looked at Karl and he at her.

"Down by that big rock is a ready-made camp," Karl was quick to say. "It has a stone fireplace and the rock cover provides good shelter from the rain. There is a creek at the bottom of the hill for water."

"May I bathe in the creek?" Douglas asked.

There was another pause as Gudrun and Karl looked at each other again.

"We have a bath tub. You are welcome to use it," Gudrun said eventually.

"A real bath tub! It sounds wonderful. Just what I need. I am covered in dust." Douglas laughed and patted at his clothing to show the dust trapped in its weave.

The three Europeans finished their polite chat as the sun lost its brilliance. Yellow invaded all colours in the failing light. The Aboriginal huts swarmed with activity as the men came in with game from their hunt. Campfires were being lit. Smoke slowly rose upward and was swept eastward, high above the mission. The birds' combined chorus signalled the end of the day.

"I'll take that bath now if that is all right with you," Douglas said.

"Yes, of course. This way," Gudrun said as she leapt to her feet. In the bathroom she gave Douglas instructions concerning the use of the unique plumbing system Karl had installed. "If you want a hot bath I'll light a fire under our laundry tub. It won't take long."

"I wouldn't dream of it. Cold water is refreshing after such a hot day," Douglas said. He went to get his pack from his horse and secured himself in the bathroom as the cold water ran from the catchment tank into the tin tub.

Karl, meanwhile, had lit the lamps in the house and settled down to read. Gudrun sat opposite her husband and took out her sewing-basket. Neither spoke.

The Maresch house was sturdily built of heavy timber and wood panel walls. The rooms were partitioned with pinewood planks over a frame. There were no ceilings; the walls went up to the roof. One large room ran across the whole front of the house, combining living, dining and kitchen areas. The back section of the house provided a bedroom and the bathroom/laundry.

Douglas began to undress in the bathroom. The sound of his boots falling heavily on the floor jarred Gudrun. She pretended not to hear anything. Soon their visitor was in the bath, lathering himself generously, splashing water all over his body. Gudrun had felt a little uneasy about it at first, but now she found herself enjoying the presence of another man in the house.

Mar-weel sat cross-legged in front of the fire with his family friends, Bobby (Gunnawulla) and Ruby (Winona). Bobby and Ruby had five children, four boys and a girl. They had come from the Warrumbungle Mountain valley area. Bobby was renowned as a great hunter. He had remarkable spear-throwing abilities, and a corroboree was composed and regularly performed in his honour. The body of the song told how he threw a solitary spear that brought down a kangaroo and pinned it to another hopping in retreat beside it — the game fed the whole clan for three days. The chorus repeated praise of him as a respected family man of the clan. One of the craftsmen had taken the bones from the paws of the two animals and fastened them to the launching section of a new woomera. He tied them securely with the well chewed guts from the animals. The woomera was ceremoniously presented to Bobby at the first performance of the corroboree in his honour. Whenever meat was in short supply Bobby would voluntarily head up the hunting party. He never returned empty-handed.

A large, curious group had come to Bobby and Ruby's camp. Mar-weel knew the people had come to hear him talk. News was a scarce commodity and storytellers were welcomed. He had news that he was not too keen on sharing but he thought it his duty to tell as many of his people as he could. Very aggressive white men were taking control of tribal lands over the mountains by any means, including murder. He told of the resistance of the Awabakal people near Newcastle. After much discussion the Awabakal had decided that they had to kill sheep for food, as and when required. After all, the white men's fences stopped all game from moving freely, so it was only just. From time immemorial hunting on this land had been their right.

But white men came early one morning and killed two families who had taken sheep. The twelve men, women and children they slaughtered were left to lie where they fell, victims of a military-style ambush.

The police and a large group of white men came to look at the results of the slaughter. No burials took place. Everyone knew who the murderers were but no action was taken against them. No more sheep were killed in the district after that but two more Aboriginal men were shot dead when they were caught travelling across a property after dark.

Five Aboriginal warriors had been revenging the killings. They burnt the homes and crops of new farmers and if they refused to leave the land they speared them. They were always on the run, but were never caught because their people protected them wherever they went.

The faces of the Kamilaroi people were tense in the firelight as they listened. They were sad to hear of traditional family land being stolen. Nobody liked the killings. Mar-weel got to his feet, stretched and strolled away, his head hung low as a quiet calm took over the camp.

When Douglas emerged from his bath, Karl guided him to the ridge behind the house to view the Warrumbungle peaks that rose so dramatically from the plains in the west. The sun had set. A cadmium red afterglow blended eerily with the cobalt blue of the sky above them. Venus had already broken through the pale sky of early night.

"Those peaks look volcanic," Douglas commented.

"They are," Karl replied. "It was a mighty force that pushed that whole area upwards. Some other areas were raised and moved on their sides."

The craggy peaks formed an impressive dark blue mass against the horizon. The lure of the mountains was strong. Douglas yearned to go there. "How long will it take to reach the base of the first peaks?" he asked.

"Timor Rock is the first real upsurge. That's about a day from here. It's on the other side of Coonabarabran."

"What's Coonabarabran like?"

"A small town. Lots of blacks. Most of them lazy good-for-nothings. There's a hotel, a post office, some churches, lots of homes. A few small farms on the edge of town, a court house and a police station."

"How many police?"

"Four full-time policemen and about five or six blacks that they recruit from time to time … you know … whenever there's trouble."

"Is there much trouble up here with the blacks?"

"Not on the mission. In town and in the camps it's another story."

"Bad, eh?"

"Yes, pretty bad. Such violence. The women are worst off. They seem to take the brunt of all the anxiety caused by European settlement here." Karl turned away as he spoke.

Douglas walked carefully to the edge of the rock and looked over. He unbuttoned the fly fold in the front of his trousers, took out his penis and began to relieve himself. Karl was uneasy and began to walk back to the house.

"It's getting dark. I'll make my way back," he said.

"All right," Douglas called over his shoulder. He watched his urine fall in a continuous stream the hundred or so feet to the ground below. He contracted the muscles at the base of his bladder. There was a real feeling of power from such a fantastic piss, he thought. He re-buttoned his fly fold, stood for a while and watched the light of the sun slowly fade. Then he walked higher up the slope to gain a better vantage point, and sat and relaxed for the first time in days, allowing his thoughts to empty out onto the vast volcanic vista in front of him.

Karl was waiting on the porch when Douglas eventually came down the slope. Gudrun could be heard inside, tending to her kitchen duties. She came out quickly when she heard Douglas speaking to Karl.

"That was spectacular," Douglas said. He looked at Gudrun as she wiped her hands on her apron.

"One can become spoilt, living with such beauty," said Karl. "You can take it for granted."

The light of the porch lamp struck the right side of Gudrun's face, clearly defining the shape of her profile. She squinted so that she might see better as she moved forward, away from the light. Carefully balancing on her toes, she manoeuvred between the two men and sat down opposite them. "Would you like to stay ... to take dinner with us?" she asked Douglas.

Karl darted a glance at his wife. She hadn't discussed this with him.

"No, I don't think so, thank you. I've already imposed too much," Douglas said. He could see the tension building between the German couple. He looked away. There was a long pause.

"You haven't imposed on us at all. Has he, Karl?" Gudrun said eventually.

"No, no … not at all. Not at all," Karl said.

"Please stay?" Gudrun asked again.

"I am rather tired. I wouldn't be very good company," Douglas said lightly. "Perhaps another time. If it is all right with you, I would like to stay on here for a short while and paint. I would like to use the mission as a base. Aboriginal people make such good subjects — maybe I'll paint some of them too."

"A wonderful idea," Karl said, holding a forced smile in place as he reached out his hand. "Good-night, then. It has been so good to meet you. Maybe tomorrow you can tell us what news you have from Europe."

"Yes, of course. Good-night," Douglas shook Karl's hand. He turned to Gudrun. "Good night." He reached for her hand and kissed it again.

Karl would talk to her later about being too informal with the stranger, Gudrun knew, but she didn't care. It was exciting.

# FIVE

Douglas stumbled his way down the slope in the dark to find Mar-weel. There was an echo of voices through the valley from the Aboriginal huts. The fires in front of each gunyah were big for cooking but small for the remainder of the evening when talking took place and stories were told. Douglas could smell the game being cooked on the fires.

"Mar-weel!" he cried out across the valley.

The large family group sitting around the fire turned as one to see the European visitor as he approached. The men stood up.

"Here, Douglas, here," Mar-weel said, getting to his feet. He walked forward to meet Douglas, to welcome him into the group, and introduced him to the men. They all sat down near the fire, the women a few yards behind but well within earshot.

"...and these are my father's friends — Bobby, and that's Ruby over there," Mar-weel was saying, smiling. Douglas shook Bobby's hand and waved and nodded to Ruby. She waved back with a friendly greeting.

"Come on, get something to eat," Mar-weel insisted as he retrieved the half-devoured kangaroo carcass from the bark platter near the fire. He carved a piece of meat from the animal and handed it to Douglas, who took it gratefully, thanking his hosts. The Kooris laughed nervously and nodded.

"This one — and this one — and this one — and this one, too, can speak your language," Mar-weel said, pointing to each man in turn, encouraging Douglas to speak to them. "The others can understand a little bit."

"Thank you for sharing your food with me," Douglas said. "You are very kind." He continued to eat as Mar-weel explained in Kamilaroi what it was that brought Douglas and himself to their country and the Warrumbungle mountains. There was an interchange of questions and more nodding as Douglas ate. A young man came up to Douglas and surreptitiously handed him a large earthen jar filled with a light-coloured beer. He looked up at the young fellow, who smiled at him and walked away. Douglas turned away from the group and took a drink from the jar. He learned that kangaroo and ale made a very tasty meal while on the road.

Later, after he had finished eating, Douglas tried to explain his oil painting method to the group. Although they were very patient with him he knew they didn't understand. He would invite those who were interested to come with him when he went on his painting expeditions, he thought. Now he was tired. He stood up and stretched. "I really have to sleep," he said. "Mar-weel, you can stay if you want. I'll be up near those rocks — apparently there's a ready-made camp area there. So I'll say goodnight."

All the men came over to shake Douglas by the hand. Some older women came up to him also, drawing giggles from the younger women, amused at their brazenness. One of the older women was mesmerised by Douglas's clear light blue eyes. She followed his gaze everywhere. Eventually they let him leave, all nodding and waving their goodnights in unison until he turned away.

Gudrun and Karl sat in the living area of their home. As Gudrun separated her woollen yarn, she could hear Douglas and his horse as he made camp, only fifty yards from the side of the house.

"I should have told him that he could sleep on the porch," Karl said in German after some time.

"You always let people bed down on the porch," Gudrun said quietly as she worked. "I was surprised you chose not to this time."

She knew full well that Karl felt himself to be in competition with the handsome stranger, and for this reason fifty yards distance was preferable to the proximity of their front porch.

Karl walked to the door, looked out and continued to speak in German. "It is a beautiful night. The moon is almost full. I think I'll take a walk."

"Very well. I'll finish here, then I'll go to bed and read," Gudrun said without looking up.

Karl would often walk at night. Sometimes he would be gone for hours, often coming home after sunrise. He strolled down the hill looking skyward. It was a clear night and the ample stars of the southern hemisphere flickered out from the wide, dark blue canopy.

Douglas settled himself onto his sleeping sack after the horse and pack were taken care of. He was tired but contented. It had been a long, hot, dusty ride from

Spring Ridge, the final leg of his planned expedition to these mysterious mountains. His journey had taken him from Sydney to Newcastle, then up the Hunter River Valley to Murrurundi, Quirindi and Spring Ridge.

Mar-weel had insisted that they collect travel stones from the bigger clans along the way. These elaborately decorated stones were gifts to travellers and acted as a passport, a talisman for safe passage to the next territory. It was a courtesy, a polite formality to be observed when travelling over tribal hunting and gathering lands. They had passed through the land of the Guringai, Dharug, Awabakal, Wanaruah and Geawegal peoples. The groups they met were always friendly once Mar-weel had displayed the stones.

Gudrun put down her sewing. Her eyes watered with strain caused by hours of squinting under poor quality light. She carried the lamp to the bedroom, sat heavily on the bed, lay back and sighed.

Douglas saw Gudrun's lamp illuminate the bedroom curtains from where he lay on his sacking. The curtains were parted very slightly and he was able to glimpse Gudrun as she walked by. He saw her shadow as she walked in front of the lamp. He supported himself on his arms as he watched her. She pulled her dress over her head and threw it on the bed then slowly took off her underwear. She stood naked, reached for her nightdress, pulled it on and went out of the frame of the window.

Douglas felt his heart pounding in his chest. He could barely contain his excitement at the sight of that silhouette of the attractive young German woman. It was totally unexpected to meet someone like her living in such a remote part of the world.

Gudrun walked past the window once more, carrying her book, and got into bed to read. Douglas lay down again, overwhelmed with weariness, and quickly fell asleep.

The Coonabarabran police came to the Belougerie camp early next morning. Four uniformed white men and three partly uniformed blacks, all on horseback. Lagging in the background, seated in a buggy, were a well-dressed white man and woman and their teenage daughter. The police woke the sleeping black people, and as they left their homes they were herded into a group. Ginny and Wollumbuy took their children in their arms and complied with the shouted instructions. The police then pushed the gunyahs to the ground, dragged the huts together with a rope behind their horses and burnt them in a huge bonfire. There was loud, almost hysterical shouting from the police as they went about their duty.

The bewildered blacks looked on in terror. Whispering quietly to each other they agreed they must be suspected of having committed a terrible crime. The police seemed to be in a frenzy.

The smoke from the burning gunyahs spiralled high into the air as the police herded the forlorn Aboriginal group into Coonabarabran for processing. It was at the police station that Ginny learned the reason for the morning's work; the young white family watching had bought the land on which the Aboriginal people were camped. The police were under instructions, contained in a hastily obtained warrant, to move the blacks away, with a government directive to relocate them at Neuberg Mission if necessary.

After Ginny's name was logged in the government directory, she decided to question the authority behind the action. She leaned forward and spoke quietly to the desk sergeant in the stone lobby of the police station. He reached over, angrily took her by the arm and pulled her roughly along a corridor that led to the cells. The door clanged loudly, ringing in her ears as he slammed it firmly shut and bolted it behind her. She sat there for what seemed like several hours. The cell became dark as night fell.

Just at the moment when Ginny feared she might never see her family again, sitting in her dark cell with tears running down her cheeks, the door creaked slowly open, spilling light in from the corridor. It was Henry Thompson, the tall, fat desk sergeant. He came in and sat on the side of her bunk. He placed a small tray holding some bread and a mug of water on the floor, then speaking quietly to her he unbuttoned his trousers and lay down beside her.

She turned her back to him, rolling away she tensed herself in a ball against the wall. He lifted her cotton dress and slowly caressed her hips and thighs, talking quietly to her all the while. She wore no underwear; she could feel his erect penis as he slowly pushed it against her buttocks. She clung firmly to the mattress. He pulled her thighs apart and thrust himself between her legs. With each thrust he probed to find her opening. He exploded in orgasm quickly after he penetrated her warm, tense body. She was too stunned to cry.

As he left the cell, another white man came in and sat next to her on the bunk. She could hear Sergeant Thompson laugh as he joined a group of men at the end of the corridor. As she realised what the rest of the night held in store for her, the tears coursed down her cheeks.

The next morning Wollumbuy and the children came to collect Ginny, as they had been told to do. The Sergeant shouted at Ginny as he ushered her to the front lobby.

"Don't you ever question anything I do in future. Do you hear?" he yelled as he pushed her forward.

Ginny cowered away from the big man as she walked down the corridor. Then she smiled as she saw Wollumbuy and the children. Pausing briefly on the steps of the police station Ginny and Wollumbuy decided they would try camping for a while at Neuberg Mission and headed in that direction along the dry, dusty Gunnedah road. There appeared to be nowhere else to go. As Ginny walked slowly alongside her family, she decided that she would never ever tell about the men who had visited her cell last night.

Douglas woke early. He could hear Gudrun as she fussed about her kitchen. He pulled himself up on one elbow and surveyed the mission in the low-angle morning light. The huts dotted the bushlands, punctuating nature. A fence ran down the roadway and a gate allowed passage through to the mission. All was empty, quiet, eerie.

In one split second Douglas found himself once again falling deep into an exciting reservoir of experience. He felt the rush of adrenalin pulse through his body. Brilliant flashes of sunlight shimmered from moisture filled leaves, creating star-burst images in Douglas's eyes. They welled with tears and he rubbed them gently. A calm level of emotion stirred the centre of his stomach. He smiled a knowing smile. Once again he had been transported by nature to another level. This was what his art was all about. If he could convey this experience to one other living person through his work, it would all seem worthwhile.

Just then Gudrun pulled back her bedroom curtains, opened the window and waved when she saw Douglas. She put her hand to her cheek and called to him. "Join us for breakfast!"

Douglas smiled and agreed. He got out of his sleeping roll, wincing momentarily as a stone pushed into his back, and quickly dressed.

Karl and Gudrun were sitting quietly as Douglas knocked on the frame of the opened door. They both got to their feet and made him feel very welcome. Gudrun had made a breakfast of freshly baked dark German bread, conserves, some cheeses and the best coffee Douglas had tasted in months. It was a typical German breakfast…

*Germany!* Douglas remembered the Mosel River Valley, the German kellers and the spectacular castles built by the mad King Ludwig. Those castles, firmly planted on rocky crags, must have been a nightmare to construct. Small wonder that the lunatic king had bankrupted his State by insisting on the completion of those marvels. Turn after turn on the Mosel and Rhine rivers, Douglas had been confronted by their magnificent monumental majesty.

"More coffee?" Gudrun offered.

"No, thank you. I really must get a move on. I want to find a good spot near the mountains this morning."

"Will you be back this evening?" she asked boldly.

"No. I plan to camp where I paint for a few days."

Gudrun was visibly disappointed. Hastily she gathered up the breakfast things and bundled them into the sink. Douglas and Karl took leave of each other while Gudrun held back at the sink. Then she turned quickly. "May I join you?" she asked.

Karl exploded. "Gudrun!"

"Please don't object, Karl. Mr Langton and I are trustworthy Christian adults. And besides, Mar-weel will be there to act as chaperone. What do you think will happen? It would be an adventure. I really want to go" — she looked directly at Douglas — "if you will take me."

"Of course I'd take you, but — "

Douglas was interrupted by Gudrun, who quickly summed the matter up. "Then it's settled."

Karl was stunned. There was a long pause. Finally Karl sat down, looked at Gudrun and suddenly smiled. He really admired his wife's forwardness and now he began to laugh uncontrollably. All three joined in. It relieved the tension.

# SIX

Douglas was surprised when Gudrun came out of her house wearing men's riding breeches. He had never seen a lady wear them before. They showed off her well-rounded hips and thighs. She carried her swag of bedding, clothing, towels and some cooking utensils and fixed it to the back of her horse. Then she mounted the horse like a man, sitting astride the saddle. Her husband smiled as he handed her two sacks of food which she secured to her saddle horn. They looked at each other and he squeezed her hand. It was an acknowledgment, permission.

"Come back safely," Karl said.

The three were soon on the road to Coonabarabran: Gudrun, Douglas and Mar-weel. It was another hot morning. Mar-weel rode ahead of Douglas, who had sweat running down his back into his shirt. Gudrun rode behind Douglas. She was fairly flushed with new-found freedom. This was excitement, this is what she had dreamed Australia could be. She noticed Douglas' wet shirt.

"Why don't you take your shirt off?" she said brazenly.

Douglas turned. "I sunburn easily. Besides, there is a lady present."

"Don't mind me. If you find it cooler, please take it off."

Douglas unbuttoned his shirt and peeled it off so that it stayed stuck into his trousers. He glanced at Gudrun who smiled back. He had a well-muscled body: he must have done some sort of manual labour, she thought. You didn't get biceps like that by painting pictures.

"Good!" she said, and meant it. It was a small act but now she felt she was in control.

They had been riding on the dusty road for three hours under the hot sun. Mar-weel rode about five hundred yards ahead of the other two, who were now riding side by side, talking as they travelled. He stopped on a rise, under a shady tree, and raised one leg over the horn of his saddle, waiting for his travelling companions to catch him up. When they got to the top of the rise they could see why he had waited. Unfolding before them was a spectacular view of the Warrumbungles. They could see along the Castlereagh river valley for miles. The distant mountain peaks took on a pale cobalt blue colour as they receded in the distant shimmering heat haze.

"Let's stop for a while," Douglas said, dismounting. He took out his water flask and offered it to Gudrun. Gladly she took a long cool drink, then gingerly climbed down from her horse. She let out an involuntary squeal as she stretched and yawned — she was slightly saddle-sore and relieved to be standing.

"Some people coming," Mar-weel told them.

About a mile down the hill was Wollumbuy and his family. When they reached Mar-weel, Gudrun and Douglas they came to sit under the same shade trees.

Gudrun was so glad to see them. "Please, have some water," she said. Gratefully they took the flask, passed it around and drank thirstily. "Are you going to the mission? Have you decided to stay with us?" she asked eagerly.

"Yes, we thought we would try it for a while," Ginny told her.

Gudrun was surprised at how well Ginny spoke. She had no accent at all.

Ginny told them how the police had moved them off their camp at the foot of Belougerie. The group laboured on in small talk until Mar-weel gave notice it was time to move on. The campsite planned for that night was still some distance away. They really should be back on the road, he suggested tactfully.

Gudrun sensed all was not well with this Aboriginal family. All the same they parted with smiles and waves, with promises of seeing each other back on the mission.

Later in the day, Mar-weel quickly established a camp on a hill near the Coonabarabran township. The lights of the oil lamps in the town were visible from the rise. The coals of Mar-weel's fire were perfect for roasting the lamb and wild yams they had brought with them. Gudrun attended to the meal with serious German gusto, much to the contained amusement of Mar-weel and Douglas.

The meal eaten, the three sleeping sacks were broken out and placed strategically around the fire.

Gudrun went to relieve herself behind some distant bushes. Mar-weel began cutting fresh saplings for use in his gunyah, he usually slept under a shelter. Douglas lay back on his sleeping-sack with his eyes closed, deep in thought.

Wollumbuy and Ginny reached the gates to the mission as the night took hold. They walked along the track that separated the shacks, the central road surveyed by Karl to divide the homes on his mission in two. It gave some aspect of formality to his *town plan*. Eventually the tired family settled on ground at the far end of the row of huts on the left. Presently, Wollumbuy walked to one of the huts, calling to its occupants as he approached. The people living in the hut came out, and so did the people next door, and the people next door to them. Soon there were many people preparing a welcome fire and food for the new arrivals.

Karl sat on the porch in the dark and watched the whole scene with a smile. The singing started, then the dancing, and Karl decided to sling his hammock on the porch. It was a balmy night with a light breeze sweeping across the valley. The smell of smoke and kangaroo flesh roasting on the fires carried to the porch. Later, in the cool evening air, Karl took his walk.

Gudrun and Douglas were laughing so hard that they woke Mar-weel from a deep sleep. He leaned out of his gunyah and began laughing as well, without the slightest idea as to what was going on. This made Gudrun and Douglas laugh even harder. Finally, each said goodnight and settled down comfortably to sleep.

Douglas enjoyed being with Gudrun; there was something between them, some magnetism. It pulled them closer each minute they were together.

Deep into the night the embers of their fire still glowed. Many nocturnal animals could be heard scurrying around their territory looking for food.

Gudrun lay awake looking at the stars for what seemed hours, then sat upright. She looked over to where Douglas lay. He heard her moving. He turned, pulled back his covers and beckoned her to come in. Without hesitation she went to his open arms and nestled under the covers. He held her tightly to his bare chest, their bodies pressed together. She could hear his heart pounding. He kissed the top of her head, breathing in her natural scent. She pulled on his shoulders with both hands. He stroked her back and neck very slowly, his hands occasionally caressing her hips.

Gudrun was overwhelmed with feelings of possessiveness. She had known when she first saw him that she wanted to be with him always, this exciting bearded stranger. She was amazed that she had fallen in love so quickly. She looked up. He kissed her lightly and she responded.

The next morning Mar-weel put a billycan of water on the regenerated fire. The sounds stirred Gudrun and Douglas, who woke at the same time. Gudrun whispered into Douglas' ear. He hugged her and kissed her lightly on the forehead.

After a breakfast of damper and tea they made their way into Coonabarabran. The town nestled strategically against the banks of the Castlereagh river.

A substantial wooden bridge was built across the river to the northern bank to link Coonabarabran by road to the mission and neighbouring Gunnedah.

Whenever anyone new came to town almost everyone came out to see. The slow parade along the main street could unnerve the most experienced traveller. At the centre of town was an intersection. The well-designed and beautifully built stone police station and Court House commanded pride of place on one corner of the new township. It stood as a monument, representing British justice in the new colony — and not only by the grandeur of its solemn architecture. Directly opposite stood the Royal Hotel, the only hostelry within a two-day ride. The Sydney mail coach stopped here. It ran twice a week and serviced the growing population housed in the many homesteads that surrounded this new agricultural district. The weatherboard post office was on the third corner and a vacant paddock, a prized development site, occupied the fourth corner of the town centre.

Douglas had directed his mail to the Coona-barrabran post office and wanted to make a stop there. He was also carrying letters and several parcels containing interesting Aboriginal artifacts that he wanted to send back to Sydney. He suggested that he should meet Gudrun and Mar-weel at the Royal Hotel after he had completed his business.

A little while later he emerged from the post office to find that a loud commotion had developed across the road at the hotel. Gudrun, he saw, was in the thick of it.

"It's their land, their country … don't ever forget that!" she was screaming loudly, forcing her voice to crack.

Douglas summed up the situation immediately. Without a word he pushed his way to the middle of the throng, took Gudrun by the arm and led her away, speaking quietly to her as they walked. Mar-weel waited on the next corner, head bent so that his chin touched his chest.

"It's indecent!" she shouted back towards the group at the hotel. Then: "Just who do they think they are?" she asked Douglas more quietly.

"I know," he said, "they just can't see."

"It's ignorance. They're scared. They don't understand and don't want to try. They think they are so superior. That drunken bunch of hooligans!"

"What actually happened?" Douglas asked. He knew it was Mar-weel they had objected to. The Aborigine was refused service by most hotels. He tried to take his place in white man's society but they would not allow it. Yet still he persisted. Douglas did his best to explain the situation to Gudrun.

"Mar-weel says that if he doesn't keep trying it will become more difficult for the younger ones, growing up in the changing world of the white men."

Gudrun was so distressed that she puffed and fumed over the hotel incident for the next fifteen miles.

Douglas pulled the mail he'd collected from the post office out of his saddle-bag as he rode slowly along the narrow trail behind Gudrun. One letter in particular, forwarded from London via Sydney to Coonabarabran, made him curious. He opened it first. It was from a respected firm of solicitors in London's Inner Temple. Hastily he scanned the copperplate handwriting of some careful clerk:

*Dear Mr Langton,*

*Regretfully, it is our sad duty to inform you of the death of your aunt, Mrs Mary Walworth, late of Old Bottersley Manor, Sussex. Your Aunt, our respected client for many years, instructed the undersigned to draft a will, witness same and lodge the warrant on her behalf.*

*We should be pleased if you would attend a reading of our late client's Last Will and Testament in these chambers at your convenience. I am bound not to reveal the scripted details of the warrant but I am able to tell you that you are the sole beneficiary of your late Aunt's substantial estate.*

*It is the understanding of this firm that while the mail system to the Australian colonies has much improved, your reply may experience considerable delays. In the meanwhile, your late Aunt's estate will be dutifully attended to, in trust.*

*We remain at your disposal, at your convenience.*

The letter was signed by Sir William Mathews, Q.C., one of the partners in the firm.

# SEVEN

The three travellers negotiated the final bend of the trail at the base of Belougerie. The topography gave no indication of what lay ahead. The magnificent rock face of the spire was vertical in places, forcing them to tilt their heads well back to view the peak.

Gudrun looked across the open field where Ginny and Wollumbuy had previously made their home. The newly arrived white settlers and their daughter had hastily erected a timber shack. Smoke plumed from the chimney as Gudrun, Douglas and Mar-weel approached. The husband was at the side of the hut chopping wood to add to the pile he was stacking in preparation for the winter. He waved as he saw the three approaching.

"Good day to you! I'm Trevor O'Neill." He smiled and offered his hand from ten yards away.

Douglas slowly dismounted and introduced Gudrun, Mar-weel and himself. He explained that they were only passing through and planned to make camp a few miles upstream.

"Please stay, we'd like the company," O'Neill said as his wife and daughter came out of the house.

Gudrun dismounted and she and Douglas walked up to the house.

"This is my wife, Maureen, and my daughter, Elizabeth," O'Neill said. "We're new to the area. We recently bought the property at a Government auction."

Mar-weel held back, not wanting to have anything to do with the family. He attended to the horses, taking them in hand and moving them to the shade of nearby trees.

The group were soon seated outdoors at a table that Trevor brought from the house. Elizabeth carried a steaming pot of tea on a tray together with cups, saucers and a small pot of honey. The mood was light and laughter was heard across the valley as the afternoon passed pleasantly away.

That evening, as Douglas and Gudrun sat in comfortable silence in front of their campfire some distance downstream from the O'Neill's, Gudrun disturbed the peaceful ambience by asking Douglas a question.

"Why do you think people like the O'Neills come out to the frontier?"

His reply was brief. "People are driven by different motives. You and Karl are here … I'm here. I'm sure the O'Neills have their reasons." He lay and watched the sky from their hastily made camp. The red of the sunset washed across the blue. On the far eastern horizon the blue slowly turned dark. A flock of white cockatoos went into a frenzy as they flew past, landing nearby in the tops of some tall gum trees.

Gudrun lay wide-eyed for hours watching falling stars, meteorites, rush across the dark clear sky. It was a warm summer night. She pulled her bed next to Douglas and as he stretched and leaned back, she slowly fell into his arms. He held her close until they fell asleep.

The next morning Douglas rose early, quickly dressed, gathered a sketch pad and some carbon pencils and went in search of compositions for his paintings. He decided to move to the high ground. It was always inspiring to look down, he thought. He pushed himself hard as he climbed, pausing occasionally to look about. His thoughts always came back to Gudrun. He wanted to be with her more than any woman he had ever known. She excited him, inspired him, he loved just looking at her, watching her move, listening to her voice. He enjoyed her ideas, how she expressed them, how clear and precise her thoughts were about the world. He was falling in love with her.

In a split second a white bolt of light flashed into his eyes. His vision became unbelievably clear. There it was, unmistakably, an amazing vista looking up the valley towards the south-west, his picture for today. He put his sketching materials down and walked a few yards to the left and then back to the right. His eyes scanned the entire landscape. He ran up the slope to allow some small bushes to become foreground for the artwork; from there his picture appeared complete. He looked at the ground about him, picked up several stones and formed them into a stack, marking the point of view for his planned painting. He sat and stared at his subject for several minutes, taking in the detail. A smile broke out on his face; he was excited. He walked to where he had dropped his sketching materials and carried them up to his vantage point and immediately began draughting.

First the composition of the major land masses had to be blocked in; the vertical lines of the trees would be added later. Douglas was expert in his technique. He had not yet told Gudrun and Karl that he had work hanging in galleries in London as well as Sydney and Melbourne — his paintings were highly respected and valuable. From his first showing at the Royal Academy in London several years ago, his work had been widely distributed by international dealers. He was a very successful artist.

Several hours passed until Mar-weel's loud, distinctive coo-ee, the bushman's call, echoed up the slope where Douglas sat working. He called back to him with two long bursts to let him know his whereabouts. Mar-weel looked up and waved. Douglas knew he would either have to go down or Mar-weel and Gudrun would come up. As he felt hungry he decided he would go down — that way he could bring his painting equipment with him when he returned. He stood and looked one more time at his subject. He felt his body freeze in that position. It was a pleasant non-movement; he felt locked into that warm freeze. It was exciting … He knew he should move, but could not, would not, just yet …

He was quite startled when Gudrun suddenly appeared beside him.

"It's beautiful," she whispered, not really wanting to intrude. They sat together quietly and Douglas began to draw. Neither of them wanted to speak. His hunger would have to wait, his work was more important. The only sound was the soft, light breeze as it pushed past the tall dry grass.

Douglas appeared sure and confident as he went about his work. He had been trained in a traditional form of painting in London, at the Royal Academy. His father would not have approved of his son's occupation, had he been alive. It would not seem manly enough to him.

Douglas' student days had been an exciting time. He lodged with Ronald Sutton, a fellow student from the Academy, in humble digs off the King's Road in Chelsea. They lived very near the Chelsea Military Barracks and soon grew accustomed to the daily routine marked by drums, bugles and bells. Every weekend he travelled home to Sunninghill to stay with his family. The family home was enormous, with acres that stretched as far as the horse paddocks at Ascot.

Douglas loved horses. Some of his earliest childhood memories were of family outings to Royal Ascot. The fields would be decorated with multi-coloured banners and the beautiful Royal Box gardens were tended all year round so that they would bloom in time for the Spring carnival. A veranda-style pavilion was built when he was very young to provide shelter for the large crowds who came to watch. It was well used when the spring rains fell. Royal Ascot would never be cancelled because of a few drops of rain.

Douglas cherished his daily walk along Chelsea Embankment to Somerset House in the Strand, the first home of the Royal Academy. (The year Douglas left England for Australia it had been moved to Burlington House, in Piccadilly.) Occasionally he and Sutton might share the cost of a hansom cab, but mostly they both enjoyed the walk. After a long day in the teaching studios they would go off to the Red Lion, a local public house. There they would share a few drinks and some food, together with their other comrades in art.

Every day after five o'clock the bar of the Red Lion quickly filled with art students. It was exhilarating. And it was there, in the middle of a very cold winter, that Douglas had first met Claudette.

After classes, Sutton and Douglas had braved the walk to the Red Lion through heavily falling snow. The warmth of the fire in the bar was inviting. As usual, the smoky bar was crowded and noisy as they pushed their way through the mass of bodies. Then Douglas saw her: Claudette Villesant, sitting deep in conversation with Hilary Beaumont, another art student. He had immediately walked over to them, and when Claudette looked up and smiled Douglas thought she was the most beautiful woman who had ever lived. Her vibrant personality seemed to soar above the noisy room.

They had talked together for the rest of the evening. About art, music, books, war, people, food ... and all too soon it was closing time. Outside in the snow Douglas asked her if she would come to the pub again the next night. She said she would.

The following evening Douglas left art class early. He was the first of his group to arrive at the Red Lion. Claudette arrived early as well. It was a repeat of the previous evening: they ate, drank and talked to the exclusion of their friends. So it went on every day for weeks, with long, boring, intolerable weekends in between.

One particular Wednesday, Douglas had left his class early as usual and found Claudette waiting in the courtyard of Somerset House. She looked agitated, upset. He ushered her quickly into the shelter of a shop doorway, where she told Douglas she had to go back to Paris. Her parents had completed the business which had brought them to London and now they were going home.

"No ... it's not fair!" Douglas said softly. He frowned, took her hand and held it to his lips while tears rolled down her cheeks. He reached out and wiped them away. He felt a dull pain swell in his chest. "Come back to my rooms," he said softly, "we can be alone there." Standing in front of the shop in the falling snow, Douglas took Claudette in his arms and they kissed. She had held him tightly as she pressed her lips against his.

They took a hansom cab to Chelsea, where Douglas ushered Claudette into his rooms, brushing the snow from her coat as he helped her to remove it. They kissed again and Claudette unpinned her long hair. Douglas ran his hands through her hair; pulling her close, he kissed her lightly. Then, in the failing afternoon light he led her to his bedroom.

The whole of that evening they spent making love. Douglas was no virgin; he had been with many Soho whores and often visited a certain fashionable house on Duke Street. But his consuming love and long withheld passion for Claudette made that particular night unforgettable. She was his first love. And she was so sexually uninhibited that she scared Douglas. He trembled with excitement; only afterwards, as they lay tightly embraced in their nakedness, could he feel relaxed. Later that night, as he escorted Claudette home, he decided that he would follow her to Paris.

The following month Douglas took leave from the Academy. His teachers had arranged introductions for him in Paris. When he arrived, Douglas visited Claudette's home near the Champs Elysees. He had met her parents briefly in London; he thought they must realise his relationship with their daughter was serious, since he had followed her to France.

Two weeks went quickly by. Douglas had not done a single stroke of work, he had not visited a single gallery or spoken to a single artist. His affair with Claudette consumed his whole life. It was Claudette who finally insisted that he meet a family friend, the artist Pierre-Auguste Renoir, who was making a reputation for himself as one of the avant-garde school of painters known as the Impressionists.

Douglas felt like a schoolboy as he walked with his work tucked under his arm, off to talk with the headmaster, off to be examined. He had achieved a lot with his painting in London, especially after his time at the Academy. He was a painter in his own right, he thought as he scurried up the steep, narrow streets of Montmartre to meet this French artist. It seemed every narrow laneway of Montmartre had a view of the Sacre Coeur. He turned a corner and walked across a small grassy square where several artists stood at their easels, painting furiously. Using the crowded sidewalk cafes, churches, bustling shoppers or house fronts around the square as subjects, they painted with serious passion. Douglas felt inspired, he was sure that somehow he belonged here.

He found number 12 Rue d'Avray and used the heavy metal door knocker that was mounted on one of the large double doors. The concierge admitted him and indicated the artist's studio at the top of the house.

He was courteously greeted by the artist; Douglas was surprised to find that he was about his own age. This Renoir had an arrogant confidence which generated an aura about him, he thought. He ushered Douglas to his studio at the top of some narrow stairs. Huge painted canvasses filled every space on the walls of the large loft. His canvasses were much bigger than Douglas liked to paint on. They were like nothing ever painted before, he thought. The colours took over the form, so that form was not so important any more. Renoir had skilfully blended the edges of his subjects into backgrounds in a glancing expression of a fleeting moment in time. Douglas was excited and smiled at Renoir as they sat and tried to communicate about painting.

Later in the day, Renoir took Douglas to a local cafe where he liked to spend his afternoons. He introduced him to his fellow artists. That day Douglas met the core of what were to become known as the French Impressionist movement. The artists Claude Monet, Edouard Manet, Camille Pissaro and Paul Cézanne were all Renoir's friends. On that particular afternoon Douglas spoke French with passion, excitedly expressing his own art in new terms. He drank red wine and ate ripe cheese, bread and olives until dark. Renoir insisted Douglas stay the night on his couch, which he did.

The next day Douglas and Claudette visited gallery after gallery looking for the works of these new friends and fellow artists; eagerly Douglas bought several paintings to be sent back to England. His remaining four months in Paris were filled with excitement and the sense of new directions, ending all too soon. Claudette was in tears as they parted. They did of course make promises and plans and wrote loving letters for months, but they never saw each other again. A few years later, Claudette married a prominent Parisian banker. Douglas graduated from the Royal Academy and had the first public showing of his works in a group exhibition. Now that his student days were over, he was aware of a vague feeling of discontent. He craved for something new. Two years later he made his decision to go to Australia.

# EIGHT

After Wollumbuy arrived at Neuberg Mission he thought he should introduce himself properly to the Pastor and made the pilgrimage to the house on the hill.

Karl lay in his hammock, thumbing through a book on vegetable gardening. He thought it would make the mission more independent if they could grow their own vegetables. The mission population so far was a long way below his expectations. He could put it off no longer: his administrators in Germany would soon begin to ask embarrassing questions. The only sure way to increase the numbers was to introduce the tenant farming scheme as laid down by the mission's British benefactor, Mr Angas. When he saw Wollumbuy approaching he clambered awkwardly to his feet.

"I'm so pleased you came back to the mission," he said, smiling.

"Well…they took us off our camp at Belougerie," Wollumbuy said slowly. "We had nowhere to go and we thought we'd give it a try here. If that's all right with you?"

"Yes, of course it is," Karl said, shaking him by the hand. He was impressed by Wollumbuy and immediately planned to recruit him to take charge of the new market gardens.

Ginny walked slowly through the dense scrub, collecting and gathering food with five other young women. The women always sorted themselves into groups of similar ages. Ginny was very experienced at gathering; often she would provide the only food for the day when she and Wollumbuy were travelling. Even though he was a good hunter, sometimes it would be days before an animal came within miles of their path. They would grow tired of eating yams but Ginny knew they would never go hungry; she could always find them their evening meal. Today she was looking for something special. She came out of the dense bush onto a freshly burnt field. There she found her friends chatting excitedly and digging furiously.

"What have you got there?" she asked.

"Bandicoot here," replied one of the women.

Ginny didn't think bandicoot came this far south. This was very unusual; it would be a delicacy indeed. She put Charlie down, jumped in the hole beside the woman she had spoken to and began to help with the digging. She used her hands until another woman handed her a stick.

Karl had taken Wollumbuy along the track that ran down to the creek behind the mission. Together they were planning where to locate the gardens. They examined the soil, sifted it through their fingers, then walked on and repeated the exercise. They had slowly and purposefully walked about a mile in the bush alongside the creek before they finally agreed on a site. Starting tomorrow, Wollumbuy would begin the mission garden project. Karl would recruit five other helpers but it would be Wollumbuy's garden. Proudly he accepted the challenge. The understanding was that he and the other five Kamilaroi men would tend the fields for thirty years. In return they would take all the food they required from those fields and live free, under government protection on the mission. Wollumbuy didn't really embrace the concept of his enslavement. He was simply happy to be an active part of the community.

He hurried back to their campsite to tell Ginny about his new role. When he got there she held up her share of the three bandicoots her group had dug out of the burrows. Both told of their exciting day and the children joined in the merriment. A happy ambience took over the campsite as it grew dark and fires were lit.

Douglas knew he was working too fast but he could barely contain himself, the excitement was so intense. Maybe it was because Gudrun was sitting watching him. He must slow down, he thought, he wasn't putting in the base detail. Hours later his anxiety level had increased. He had to stop to evaluate his work. He wiped his brushes and stepped back, giving his eyes a moment to readjust, then he heaved a huge sigh of relief. The painting was good, he knew it. He had succeeded once again. He had no idea how it happened — maybe it was a gift from God. A warm glow of excitement swept through his body. Confidently he went back to his canvas and lightly, even lovingly, added the fine finish that artlovers looked for in his work.

Gudrun lay back in the warm summer sun. The sky was so blue it was as though Douglas had stroked his paint-filled brush over it, she thought. She wondered what Karl was doing at this precise moment. He was a creature of habit and routine and liked to know what was in store each day — his agenda, he called it. "Let's see, what's on our agenda for today?" he would say every morning. Gudrun did not enjoy having her life being so well planned and organised, it didn't leave anything to chance. She liked taking chances. *Fate, where were you when I married Karl?* she asked silently. Gudrun was a fatalist. She hadn't thought of Karl at all since she left the mission. This afternoon she couldn't stop thinking of him. She counted up the days. It was Friday, so Karl would be at the mission church going over his notes for the Sunday service.

Karl and Wollumbuy were in a lather of sweat, preparing the new missionary gardens. Karl took off his wide-brimmed hat and wiped his brow as he looked at the parcel of land that he and Wollumbuy had staked out that morning. Wollumbuy was not as affected by the heat as Karl, but fluid still left his body as his work rate increased under the summer sun. He stopped working to take a drink from the water bucket. He looked farther upstream along the creek to see how the other Aboriginal men were faring in their efforts to clear the ground. They were all doing a fair share, he thought. He took up his sharp scythe, resumed his established rhythm and continued to mow down the tall dry grass.

"Can you see it?" Karl asked Wollumbuy.

"I *can* see it, Pastor Maresch," Wollumbuy said proudly sharing Karl's vision.

"I can almost taste it," Karl said softly.

Wollumbuy broke into convulsive laughter and grabbed at his tensed-up stomach muscles, feigning that he was in pain. "Taste it?" he exclaimed. "No, you can't taste it!"

"Yes, I can, I tell you. I can taste it." Karl joined in the joke. He broke into a chuckle as they both sat down and took a well-earned rest.

Later, in the cool of late afternoon, Karl went to the mission church. He sat on a bentwood chair at the desk beside his pulpit, opened his Bible and began to read. He stared for some time at the page at which he had opened the book. Quickly he made some notes, closed the Bible, leaned back, closed his eyes and began meditating. He clasped his hands together, interlocking his fingers. Fifteen minutes later he stirred and without hesitation went back to his note-taking. He was refining his sermon for Sunday.

Presently it grew dark. Karl set aside his papers and lit the large candle on the table. He missed Gudrun, she brought so much vitality to his life. He remembered how she had looked when their ship reached Sydney Harbour, two years ago. So excited, so animated. How could anyone be as excited as that, he wondered: certainly he could not. She embraced all his ideas with enthusiasm. She was devoted to him, his work, the church. I do understand her and I do trust her, he thought. She has the need to fly occasionally, and I know I must not cage her in — but I wish she were here with me now.

The interior of the church appeared different in the candlelight. The high timber walls took on an orange glow, the shadows shimmered and flickered as the flame danced with the slightest movement of air. Karl used Sundays as a celebration of the mission's survival of another week. He desperately wished that Gudrun was back home to share in his celebration this week.

Karl left the church and began the short walk up to his house. The Aboriginal huts were vibrantly alive with children running all around them. They played all day long, Karl thought. He wondered if he and Gudrun should have a child. He liked children. They could teach the infant, raise it here on the mission and later send it back to Germany for finishing school. His family would assist in that. His family would be proud of his child. Yes, they should have a child. Proudly he strode up his steps, onto his porch and into his empty house.

The canine chorus in the Aboriginal camp yapped a sequence of harmonies as Karl sat alone and ate his hastily prepared dinner. He was a practical, efficient man who liked everything in order. He had cooked a kangaroo stew and measured equal portions to serve him for three days. All he had to do was add dumplings on each occasion and dinner was ready — no fuss, no ceremony. He did not stand on ceremony when he was alone, but he insisted that good manners be practised in company. Karl was proud that Germans were considered to be such a civilised people. The kangaroo stew tasted even better than yesterday, he thought. He was running out of bread. Gudrun cooked special German bread for them. I must learn her secret, he thought.

He was aware that Gudrun held many secrets. When she returned from the painting excursion with Langton he would not intrude on those secrets. She would tell him what she thought he should know. Karl put his boots on in preparation for his walk. Tonight he planned a long trek.

Mar-weel had been missing all day. He had not told Douglas what he would be doing. This was not unusual: he often walked off deep in thought, and he always returned. But Gudrun began to show concern when it became dark.

Douglas prepared a fire while Gudrun opened a sack of food and took out flour, salt and sugar.

"*Coo-ee!*"

The bush call startled Gudrun. It was Mar-weel. He was still a long way off judging by the sound of his call. Squinting in the failing light, Gudrun thought she could make out someone on the other side of the river. Something *was* moving over there, she thought…

"*Coo-ee! … Coo-ee!*" Douglas replied, raising his head to the sky.

Out of the darkness strode Mar-weel, carrying a row of fish strung onto some bush rope fashioned from long grass. He had a big smile on his face; his teeth glowed in the firelight.

"Fish tonight, Douglas!" he called out. He approached the camp like a shy child seeking praise.

"Well done, Mar-weel!" said Douglas, jumping to his feet. "How did you get them?"

"Easy," Mar-weel replied. "With traps, Baiame traps."

"What are … Baiame traps?"

"Haven't I told you the story of Baiame traps?" Mar-weel said in mock surprise. He knew quite well that he had not.

"No, my friend, you haven't." Douglas reached out and took the fish from Mar-weel. "You can tell us later, just give me those beauties here." He took the fish off the twine. There were six, each one meal-size. After he had cleaned them he wrapped the fish and tied them tightly in strips taken from a nearby paperbark tree. He then placed them deep beneath the hot coals of the fire. This traditional Aboriginal method he had learned from Mar-weel months previously. Gudrun added to the repast with a batch of seasoned dumplings boiled in a pot placed on top of the hot coals.

Sitting back after their meal, Gudrun said, "Mar-weel, I want to know about those Baiame traps. Come on, tell us."

Mar-weel smiled and began to tell the legend as it was told to him…

*The Story of Baiame and The Stone Fish Traps:*

*Baiame is the great All-Father. He shaped the world, creating the natural features you see around you. He created all the important features in Aboriginal culture. He once lived here on earth but then he went into the sky, from where he now watches. He still comes to earth today to attend the Bora ceremonies.*

*He is married to two wives and has several sons. He is something like us but he has magic ways. He can do anything and sees everything. He watches over his people. Aboriginal people can always feel his presence.*

*A big drought came during the early creation time. All the areas around here that usually had lots of fish suddenly had none. The whole land turned brown from baking in the sun. When the rivers dried up all that were left were little* green water-holes. All things began to die — the trees, the bushes, the grass. The animals that remained became stuck in the mud surrounding the reduced lakes and water-holes and were speared by hungry hunters. The sun swallowed the last of the waters. A terrible famine followed.

Baiame saw the suffering and came back to earth with two of his sons. The sons lifted the scattered boulders and stones that were dug up by Baiame and set them in the pattern of a great fish-net. Using the big boulders first, then the smaller ones, the net was built. Baiame showed how to open and close the traps securely at either end by moving the key stones. He insisted the people maintain the trap in good repair.

That night the people performed a corroboree in Baiame's honour. Later Baiame showed them how to call rain. Hours of dancing in the dirt and the dust with their feet made the dust rise into the sky. The exhausted dancers fell and slept but were soon wakened by huge raindrops falling on their naked bodies.

Day after day the rains came down from the sky and washed the green water away. The river water rose slowly and spilled down into areas that a few days ago were totally dry. Before their eyes the people saw the water run into Baiame's trap: looking more closely, they could see thousands of fish swimming in the new trap. The water spilled over the traps and ran farther downstream but the fish remained.

The excited people jumped into the still waters of the trap and herded the fish into a corner, then killed them with sticks or short spears. The bream, or black grunter as Aboriginal people call them, were named after the grunting sound they made when Baiame first speared them.

*The old, wise men made sure the stones were securely fastened so the fish couldn't escape and warn other fish about Baiame's trap.*

"My friend told me there were Baiame traps up this river so I went off to look for one," Mar-weel said. Then he lay down, content that he had told the story well.

# NINE

Douglas placed his two recently completed paintings against a large sandstone boulder and scanned them with a critical eye for an hour before Gudrun insisted he come and have breakfast. She had prepared tea and damper as Mar-weel packed the gear and secured it on their horses. This morning they were heading back to the mission.

The sky was clear and deep blue above them. It shimmered light blue at the horizon, indicating another hot day ahead. Mar-weel observed that on their trip here they had actually come in a wide curve. He suggested they take another trail over the high plateaux to the mission. They found out later that the high trail actually cut more than a day off the journey. Gudrun was very talkative as they rode, Douglas was preoccupied. He was thinking about London and his Aunt's inheritance.

The sun was low in the sky when they turned their horses through the mission gate. Karl ran down the hill to greet his wife. His arms were wide open, over-gesturing in wild enthusiasm to receive her. Gudrun went to him smiling and they hugged tightly.

"Come ... tell me about your adventure," Karl said as he took her heavy pack from her. They walked slowly to the house. When they got to the steps Gudrun turned.

"Douglas, Mar-weel, come on!" she called.

"No, you go ahead," Douglas said, respecting their privacy. "Mar-weel wants to join his friends' camp and I'll take my old spot over there." He waved and retreated to the rock beside the house.

Douglas welcomed the night. He needed to feel the veil of darkness over him so that he could become anonymous. He wanted to become lost in his thoughts, allow his ideas and plans to rise to the surface. Modern city life made more demands on people, he thought. He cherished his time in the outback — especially now, as he turned over his plan to go to London. The worst part was not knowing if he would ever return.

Mar-weel was woken from a deep sleep by a thudding kick in the back.

"Get up, mate, you're coming with us," the dark, shadowy form above him said loudly.

Bobby and Ruby and others from huts close by came to see what the commotion was about. Three white policemen, five Aborigines partly clothed as policemen and their horses surrounded Mar-weel as he rose to his feet.

"What's wrong? What have I done?" Mar-weel asked indignantly.

"You *know* — what you've done," one of the policemen answered.

Sergeant Thompson leaned back on his horse. He nodded to the black policemen and they moved towards Mar-weel.

"No, I d— " Mar-weel was cut short by a rifle butt to the side of his neck. He fell heavily to the ground. Two black policemen started kicking him and hurling obscenities. Bobby was restrained by Ruby. The crowd didn't like this; they began to chastise the police verbally. One old woman came forward and helped Mar-weel to his feet. He was bleeding heavily from a split lip and had a wide gash at one side of his head. She was pushed roughly to one side as a rope was tied around Mar-weel's neck and he was led away.

Bobby sent his eldest boy up the slope to wake Douglas and explain what was happening to Mar-weel. Quickly Douglas dressed and followed the boy as he ran through the mission gates and up the Coonabarabran trail.

When he saw the police ahead Douglas called: "Hey, up there! Stop! What's the matter?"

"Stay out of this, mister," one of the mounted policemen told him. "This one's no good. He's a killer."

"No, you're wrong! I know this man," Douglas insisted.

The big Sergeant refused to listen to him. "Then you're lucky he didn't do you in, too. This black's a murderer, understand, a bloody killer. He speared and cut up the young O'Neill family in their house at Belougerie. He had to leave in a hurry and his Aboriginal stuff was lying all over the place. Now he's going to pay for what he did."

Douglas was dumbfounded. Trevor, Elizabeth and Maureen O'Neill, *murdered*? He refused to be fobbed off. He explained that he had hired Mar-weel in Sydney and would be taking him back there when he returned, that he had been with him constantly every day.

"You can swear that he has been with you every hour of every day during that time?" the Sergeant demanded.

Douglas felt he had found a chink in the big policeman's armour, that he was weakening ... then he remembered the day Mar-weel had gone missing at Belougerie, the day he went to look for Baiame's fish-traps.

"Well, not every minute of every day, but —"

"Look, we have an eye-witness who saw him one mile from the house on the day of the murders and that's good enough for me." The Sergeant was determined. He ruled this territory. He would do it his way. He was sure. "Now, get out of the way, nigger lover, you're interfering with police business here."

Douglas could not believe it. He stood in a trance as the police led Mar-weel away. Soon they had disappeared into the darkness.

Early next morning, Gudrun and Douglas went at half-gallop for the whole journey to the police station at Coonabarabran. After much persistence they were allowed to see Mar-weel in his cell. As the door opened Gudrun gasped and turned away. Mar-weel was hanging from the iron grid built into the small high window of the cell. He had his own shirt tied tightly around his neck.

It was Sunday, Karl's day of celebration. Gudrun would not be with him today after all; she had remained in town at the police station with Douglas. Karl's Sunday church service always began on time.

As Douglas and Gudrun drew near the mission on their return journey they could hear singing. Ahead of them the trees briefly held the sounds, then in a fraction of a second they transferred the song to a nearby cluster. They had ridden most of the journey back from town in stunned silence. Finally Douglas spoke. "I have to go to England," he said abruptly.

Gudrun stopped her horse and looked at him. "I thought you were here for some time, to paint?"

"That was my original plan but I've changed my mind. I have received a letter — it has taken months to get to me. It seems I have inherited a substantial estate. My Great-Aunt has died."

"Oh, my God." Gudrun felt empty. Until this moment her life had become full to overflowing. Now it was empty. A dull void blocked all thoughts in her head.

"I have to go to London in order to claim my inheritance," Douglas explained.

"When ... when will you go?"

"I don't know ... soon." Douglas knew that wasn't a fair reply.

"Oh," Gudrun said softly.

They rode on in silence to the mission as the sound of another hymn was relayed through the tall gum trees.

Children ran and played outside the church as people began to leave. Karl walked through the throng and stood at the entrance to shake his parishioners by the hand as they left his weekly celebration. He saw Gudrun and Douglas ride through the gates together.

Gudrun made tea for Karl, Douglas and herself on the house porch. She told Karl how she and Douglas had sworn an affidavit for the police, verifying that Mar-weel could not be responsible for the horrible murders of the O'Neills because he had been with them at the time. On the day of the fishing, the day the murders were committed, he had returned to camp with his magnificent catch with no sign of distress, not a speck of blood upon him. The police had finally agreed to seek out the real culprit or culprits after they accepted their affidavit. They acknowledged the death of Mar-weel as a mistake, a tragedy, but they shrugged their shoulders as they spoke.

The following week Karl rose very early one day. It was time for him to ride his parish boundary. This he did alone every two months. It usually took him five or six days. He was a little concerned that Douglas was still at the mission, but he trusted Gudrun.

He enjoyed visiting the white families in the district, bringing the breath of Christ to many people living on the western plains. Last year he had ridden through a treacherous bushfire so that he could reach a family in time for a burial on their property. Karl was a very committed missionary.

He placed a note on Gudrun's dresser and quietly left. It was written in German:

*My loving wife,*

*I did not want to disturb you from your sleep. It is time for me to visit my parish again. I will ride south to Ulamambri and back along the Tambar Springs trail. I will be back before Sunday. When I return I want us to try to conceive a child.*

*Your Husband, Your servant, Karl.*

Wollumbuy didn't care much about the sun as long as he had enough water to drink through the day. There was work to be done in the garden and there was nothing to be gained by delaying it just because it was so hot. It was always hot in the summer. He had heard a lot about growing food, and he wanted to understand how it was done.

After a great deal of back-breaking work the whole area was now cleared. Karl said it was about four acres in size and he decreed that it would be divided into three lots. He wrote it down on a chart and hung it on a wall at the mission school.

*THE MISSION GARDEN*

*Lot 1 — peas, beans, onions, capsicum and spinach. Fertilise with compost and animal manure.*

*Lot 2 — potatoes, beets, carrots and parsnips. Add newly blended mixture of fertilisers to this crop.*

*Lot 3 — cabbages, pumpkin, sprouts and broccoli. Use a mixture of lime and blended fertilisers on these.*

At the bottom of his chart he wrote:

*Commencing from now, each vegetable group will be rotated annually to the adjoining plot, returning every three years to its original lot.*

Karl declared his system would avoid destroying the land. He verified the rotation method from his reading of two books sent to him from the Lutheran administrators in Germany.

Wollumbuy was careful not to plough too deeply as he made furrows for the seeds. They were to be sown next week, but first the soil had to be aerated for a short time. He was excited by this science of food growing. It gave him the sort of power that was usually reserved for the shaman.

On this day Ginny began vomiting. She wasn't sure what had caused it but her stomach ached and she dared not move. She didn't really believe that evil spirits invaded your body to make it hurt. She knew that some food or water could make people fall ill.

Wollumbuy came home exhausted. When he found that Ginny was ill he asked for a little offering of food from the next camp. He took the children for a walk after they had eaten; this allowed Ginny to suffer in private. They came back quietly in the dark then all the family settled down and fell asleep in their cosy bark gunyah. Two grey owls hooted in the trees overhead as the campfires burnt themselves out.

Karl could barely see the small two-room house ahead through the drifting smoke from the burning tree stumps. Brian Lumsden had been clearing and burning and ploughing for weeks. He knew he would spend the next two years preparing the land to plant his wheat. They already had a vegetable garden, fifty sheep, about twenty hens and a couple of roosters, three cows and a bull. His wife, Helen, was an unusual woman, Karl thought. He remembered how she had enjoyed his account of his adventures at sea on his journey to Australia. She sat wide-eyed like a child. She had been born here in the north-west country and had never seen the ocean.

He could see Helen walking at the back of the house but Brian was nowhere in sight. He must be away clearing and burning, Karl thought. Helen waved when she saw Karl approaching.

"How are you, Helen?" Karl asked, smiling.

"Thank you, I am well," she answered.

"Where's that good man of yours?" Karl asked jokingly. "Is he off drinking in town again?"

"No, he is in the third field, over there." Helen Lumsden pointed into the distance. "Come down … I'll put on a pot of tea."

# TEN

Douglas sat and sketched the whole day away. It was his habit to immerse himself in his work when he was troubled. Gudrun came by late in the day to bring him a cool drink made from freshly squeezed lemons. She sat with him briefly and very formally asked him to dinner. He was a little taken aback by the formality with which she delivered the invitation but he readily agreed.

He arrived on Gudrun's porch scrubbed and cleaned after a long swim in the creek. The leeches proved a nuisance but the water was very refreshing after a hot summer's day. Gudrun met him at the door. She was wearing a new dress for the occasion, of light yellow cotton, the bodice pulled tight across her breasts; the full skirt, gathered at her waist, fell to her ankles. She wore her hair up. She took him by the arm and led him to the couch.

"Let me get you something cool to drink."

She went quickly to the kitchen and began filling two glasses from a blue-and-white porcelain pitcher. Douglas walked behind her. He looked at the care she had taken in decorating the table. It was laid beautifully with linen, china, silver, a centre-piece of wild flowers in a huge vase and two lighted candles. He felt tongue-tied.

"It's ... beautiful," he said after some time.

"Thank you."

"And so are you." He came behind her and squeezed her around the waist, kissing her lightly on the neck. She turned, pulled him close and he kissed her long and deep.

"Please," she said, "it's becoming more difficult to control."

"I know. Don't you think I'm having trouble too?" Douglas whispered softly. "You look so beautiful ... we are alone ... I'm here at your invitation. It's difficult for me as well, you know."

"Please, let's sit down. I just wanted us to enjoy what time we have left," Gudrun said. The words came from her mouth, she heard them, but it was as if someone else had said them.

Douglas did not know what to do. He knew he had to go to London. He knew he would be gone for years. Gudrun was married to a man he liked and admired, but he knew he loved her as he had loved no other woman, not even Claudette. She made him feel complete just by being near her.

She brought the cool lemonade on a tray. She moved with such poetic poise, he thought. They sat and talked as two well-mannered, moral Christian adults should, each suppressing their mounting physical passion.

Gudrun served a meal of lamb and vegetables and struck out a bottle of the fine German wine that Karl reserved for special occasions. Douglas felt an overwhelming passion rise in him. It could have been the vision of Gudrun, her face glowing in the candlelight, or it could have been the effect of the wine, but Douglas knew that if he didn't act now he could regret it for the rest of his life.

"I'm sorry, I tried," he said, then stood up and reached for her with both arms, pulling her to her feet. She threw her arms around his neck and kissed him. At that moment neither of them cared for Christian principles or social morality. They would deal with rational behaviour later — tomorrow, next week. For the rest of that evening they were consumed by their overwhelming passion for each other.

Karl tied his horse to the post near the door of the Lumsden house, dusted himself down and went inside. It was a simple settler's hut, with basic practical furnishings. They hadn't made any improvements to it since he had been here last. He knew they were too intent on getting the land cleared. Karl always felt welcomed by the Lumsdens and always included them on his southerly ride twice a year. Over the teacups Helen became very talkative; she was understandably lonely. Karl listened with interest to her stories of how she coped with life on the remote farmland. Presently Karl took some Aboriginal artifacts from his bags and placed them carefully around the room, discussing their significance with Helen. Two hours passed. Then Brian came through the door. He was pleased to see Karl and shook his hand. He invited the Pastor to spend the night in his home, and Karl politely accepted, as was usual.

The sun set quickly. Due to the cloudless sky, there was a very short twilight. Helen served a simple meal of mutton stew and potatoes with fresh bread. Karl was asked to say grace before dinner. Afterwards there was some brief talk, then it was time to settle down to sleep.

"We need our sleep," Brian said with a smile. But he really meant it. He worked so hard every day.

Helen made a bed for Karl on the floor. The lamps were blown out and they all retired.

Karl lay on his back, his eyes wide open. He could hear the couple shifting on their mattress, adjusting themselves for sleep. Sometime later, he rose from his bed and walked out of the house. The night animals scampered about the field as he closed the door. He walked fifty yards from the house and fell to his knees to pray.

When he returned, he closed the door quietly and reached for the nulla-nulla — a huge Aboriginal club — he had placed in one corner of the room. He walked into the next room: there, in the moonlight streaming through the window, he clearly saw the Lumsdens asleep on their bed. He raised the club over his head and brought it down with tremendous force upon Brian's head. His skull sounded like a dry hollow log as it cracked under the force of the blow. Brain tissue sprayed out over the bed and onto the side of Helen's face. She awoke in a fit of confusion. Karl raised the nulla-nulla again and looked coldly into her pleading eyes. Her loud, high-pitched screams filled the small room with terror as he brought the heavy club down. She managed to bring her left arm up to protect her head but her forearm crunched easily when the club hit, pushing her arm into her head. The bones of her forearm penetrated her skull at the left temple and came out on the other side behind her right ear. Blood sprayed everywhere, flowing along the folds in the sheets and falling into pools on the floor.

Karl threw the club against the wall. He paused, and looked about the room several times as he breathed in deeply. He pulled Brian off the bed, dragged him to the front door and pushed him backwards away from it so that he landed flat on his back. Although Karl had hit him hard there was very little blood coming from Brian's head. Karl wanted people to discover Brian's body here. He wanted them to think that Brian had answered a knock at the door and was attacked immediately upon opening it.

Karl then went back to the bed and climbed onto his knees beside Helen's body. He rolled her over onto her back and roughly ripped the front of her nightdress. Her young, well-rounded body was totally exposed. He opened her legs wide apart and positioned himself on his knees between them. Then he produced an Aboriginal phallic object from his pocket and forced it roughly between her legs. He began violently pushing it in and out of her, again and again, faster and faster, ramming it hard into both of her openings. Sweat was streaming from his face and his bulging eyes never blinked. Finally, exhausted, he left the blood-covered twelve-inch long phallus inside her for others to find. He threw the remaining Aboriginal objects randomly around the two rooms. He would burn his blood-soaked clothes, bathe in a creek and put on fresh garments before going home. Calmly, Pastor Karl Maresch gathered his belongings together and left.

Gudrun lowered herself into the hot bath and allowed the water to carry her away. She lay back, closed her eyes and relaxed. Slowly she began to rub her thighs. She leaned back, allowing her head to go partially underwater until her ears were totally submerged. She tapped the bottom of the tin tub with her finger nails — it was a game she played. Suddenly she heard other strange sounds she couldn't account for. She sat upright, sweeping back her long wet hair. Outside she heard yelling and screaming. Quickly she dried herself, pulled on a wrapper and hurried onto the porch.

At the gates of the mission a band of chained Aboriginal men was being led by police into the mission grounds. The prisoners were bound at the neck by large key-locks in chain links. They were connected to each other. It was a gruesome sight.

Douglas was already there, talking to Thompson, the big police sergeant. By the time Gudrun reached them the policemen had begun unlocking the chains.

"They say this action has been introduced to combat the spate of recent homestead murders," Douglas told Gudrun as she took his arm.

"Just how many murders have there been? Did they say?" she asked with a frown.

"Thirty," Douglas replied. He lowered his head.

"What!" Gudrun was visibly shocked.

Sergeant Thompson rode back to where they were standing and told them that Pastor Maresch knew they were rounding up the blacks and bringing them here. He said Karl supported the government view and offered the mission's full cooperation. The Sergeant laughed and added: "He said it would

87

improve his mission numbers and impress the Germans back home."

Gudrun went red with rage. "I don't believe you!" she shouted.

The Sergeant shouted back. "I don't care very much what you believe, Mrs Maresch. We're leaving these blacks here in the care of your husband's mission. As of today they have been catalogued by us and are now officially wards of the state. They must remain on the mission grounds — they cannot leave without your husband's permission. This was all arranged with your husband weeks ago." He turned and called to his men. "Come on, let's get out of here."

The police left the prisoners sitting on the grass at the entrance to the mission. They were all male. Douglas, shocked, raised his eyes to the heavens as the forty forlorn Aborigines began talking amongst themselves. They looked half-starved.

Bobby emerged from the group of mission Aborigines gathered there. He walked up to where Douglas and Gudrun were standing and asked very slowly and deliberately: "What is going on here? These men are enemies of my people — they can't stay here."

"There is nowhere else for them to go," Gudrun told him. Then, bewildered by her answer, she grimaced. In a country as big as Australia there was nowhere else for these people to go?

Suddenly the problem was solved. The mission Aborigines came forward, embraced the prisoners, their traditional enemies, and took them into their care. That night, around a huge bonfire, the large gathering of different Aboriginal clans were united in song and dance — forced to live together by a central government authority.

"I feel nervous," Gudrun told Douglas as they sat watching the huge corroboree from the porch.

"Do you want me to stay?" he asked her.

"No, not tonight." Reaching out, she took his hand and squeezed it. Sounds of their traditional songs filled the valley as flames from the fire forced sparks and embers to fly high into the clear dark sky.

Karl arrived home early next morning. He startled Gudrun as he woke her from a deep sleep. He sat on the side of the bed and kissed her on the forehead. For a split second she thought it was Douglas — she hoped it was Douglas.

Immediately they took up a habitual routine, as married couples often do. The ritual allowed each to adjust back to one another. The small talk, the posturing, various displays of undress, nakedness, the short, familiar passionless kisses as they passed close by each other: for the first time it all felt contrived to Gudrun. We *always* behave this way, she thought as she left the bedroom. She avoided the question of conceiving a child.

"I'll make a pot of tea," she called from the kitchen. "Would you like me to heat a warm bath for you?"

"I'll have some tea, then I'm going to the church for prayers. I'll have a bath afterwards, thank you, my dear," Karl called back in German.

The routines, rituals and courtesies of their marriage were there for a reason, she thought — they were there because she and Karl did not really know each other, even after four years of marriage. We don't allow ourselves to behave openly and honestly towards each other, she told herself. We parade around in a life fashioned from polite Prussian culture. As for our sex life … Gudrun knew now that she needed her aroused sexual appetite satisfied by more than the episodic, twice-yearly indulgence she experienced with Karl. She knew it was difficult for him: his religious convictions tightly reined in his passion, but she found it very hard to receive his pent-up lust when he finally allowed it to be released.

Karl had planned their lives on his personal interpretation of theology and philosophy: now Gudrun felt that she wanted to broaden the parameters. She had new questions that demanded answers. Had Karl actually entered into an agreement with the authorities to take Aboriginal prisoners onto their mission? Was his prime consideration for the mission to grow at all costs? Did he fully understand the harsh reality of raising a child of their own on the mission? If he was unable to answer these questions satisfactorily she would have to rethink her role in his master plan. Gudrun frowned, deep in thought as she went about her duties.

They had tea together, then Karl prepared himself to go to the church to pray. Gudrun had noticed that he always had a long prayer session when he returned from his parish visits. She decided to go to the church with him. Walking down the slope in front of the house, they could see Douglas. He was sitting on top of a rocky outcrop, sketching. They both waved to him.

"Karl, while you were away I was asked to take custody of forty starving male Aboriginal prisoners from the Coonabarabran police. They said you had arranged it with the government, is this true?" Gudrun could no longer contain herself; her loaded question exploded from her lips.

"Yes. It is true," Karl said abruptly.

They stopped and faced each other.

"How could you! Do you think this is the way to treat the people here — to keep them unwillingly locked up on your mission? Is this godly? Is this right?" Gudrun was angry. Karl stared at his wife wide-eyed as she continued: "Does it sit well with your conscience? I must tell you it does not do so in mine." Tears welled up in Gudrun's eyes as she continued softly, "Do you really expect me to have your baby and raise it here on your mission-prison?"

Karl frowned *What had he done,* he thought. It was too late; he could not turn back now. Gudrun would have to agree to support his actions — after all, she was his wife. She always obeyed if he applied enough pressure.

"How dare you!" he screamed at her. "Go to the house immediately! I will discuss this with you later."

For the first time Gudrun feared her husband. She shuddered and began to shake uncontrollably. She turned away and walked back with great determination to the house.

# ELEVEN

The garden had become a thing of wonder at the mission. Wollumbuy had been elevated in status because of it. He enjoyed his new position. Pastor Maresch had promised that the new food would take only a short time to grow and he was right. Intrigued by the scientific methodology employed in the growing of food, Wollumbuy soaked up the information with an inner smile.

Karl arranged for a wholesale produce buyer to visit the mission gardens with a view to entering into a long-term contract to buy their burgeoning crops. Masterton, the buyer, travelled the state for two months of each year building up his list of suppliers. He was a tall man with a limp, the result of a dislocated hip. He wore fancy city clothes and rode in a buggy.

Wollumbuy was nervous when he was told that a buyer was coming; he set about tending his plants with a fervour Karl had not seen before. At last, the brightly painted maroon-and-yellow buggy steered through the mission gates. As the stranger got down, Wollumbuy put his tools away, wiped his soiled hands and went for a closer look. Light rain began to fall as he watched from beneath a group of trees. He understood how the buyer would store and sell food at the markets for money, but what he couldn't quite come to terms with was that white people would work at jobs they often hated to earn enough money to buy the food — the basis of the whole monetary system.

Karl and Gudrun, though under strain privately in recent weeks, put on a united front publicly. Wollumbuy watched as they welcomed Masterton into their house. Rain ran down Wollumbuy's hair and onto his face. Eventually, Karl emerged from the house and led the buyer down to the gardens. Wollumbuy still maintained his distance, not quite within earshot. They laughed a lot, he thought. He hoped that was a good sign.

The buyer plucked a solitary bean from its stem, then broke it open and tasted it. He looked at Karl and smiled his approval. Karl was confident, he knew they had grown a high quality crop. Masterton checked the other vegetables; each met with his approval. Karl picked a selection of each variety and placed them in a sack. Then they made their way back to the house. As they walked by Wollumbuy, Karl pointed him out, saying something to the stranger, who smiled and waved.

Wollumbuy decided to wait outside the house. Rain was still falling lightly. It was several hours later when Masterton, Karl and Gudrun came onto the porch. They said their goodbyes and the buyer limped over to his buggy, reined the horse in and steered him through the gates. Karl called to Wollumbuy to join him on the porch.

"He loved it all, Wollumbuy." He reached out and shook Wollumbuy by the hand. "Congratulations. We've done it! He wants us to harvest our crop early, pick everything immediately."

"That's good," Wollumbuy said, trying to keep his excitement under control.

"We have only two problems to overcome. Firstly, we have to pick and crate it ourselves; secondly, we have to cart it at our expense to the markets in Sydney," Karl told him.

Wollumbuy was in the garden early the next day. Every muscle in his body ached and he was thirsty. His eyes stung sharply from the sweat that ran into them. Taking a rag from his back pocket he wiped his face. He liked hard work. He turned to see the gleaming sunlight dancing on the surface of the clear waters of the creek. It was too inviting — and they had been working for a long time. He laid down his mattock, called to his fellow workers and they went eagerly towards the coolness offered by the fast-running waters.

Quickly ridding themselves of their scant clothing, the men dived, jumped and fell into the water. Wollumbuy enjoyed diving underwater and swimming submerged until his air ran out. He did it again and again. The current swept him away downstream. Floating in the centre of the strong current, he allowed his weightless body to travel around several bends in the creek before he swam to shore. As he clawed his way up the slope he noticed something gleaming in the steeply banked wall. He went over for a closer look, dug it out and took it to the water's edge to wash it. The shining yellow stone glowed as he wiped off the last pieces of dirt.

Wollumbuy had heard about yellow-stone fever. White men went crazy trying to get their hands on such stones, then they sold them for a great deal of money.

He looked again at the shining rock, holding it in both hands. It was almost as big as his foot. It was heavy, he thought, heavier than most rocks. He wondered how much money he could sell this stone for. *Gold* — that was what they called it, he remembered.

His co-workers were still laughing and splashing in the shallow waters near the bank. One of them looked up to see Wollumbuy walking towards them carrying the heavy yellow stone.

"What have you found, Wollumbuy?" he called.

Everything went quiet by the creek as the men gathered round to see Wollumbuy's prize.

"Is it really the yellow stone?" asked a tall young garden worker in his native Kamilaroi tongue.

"I'm sure it is," Wollumbuy said. "Don't tell anyone where it came from — there may be more stones here for us to find, and we'll get the money when we sell them." He tore some bark strips from a nearby paperbark tree and wrapped the stone in them, then he quickly walked back to his camp to prepare for the walk to town, where he would try to sell it.

The white-flowering gum trees bloomed throughout the wooded areas near the mission. To Douglas, they seemed to have appeared overnight. He took his painting case and some small canvasses with him on a ten-minute walk into the dense scrub near the mission. He found the undergrowth fascinating. The discoloured fallen branches with high grasses and lower-growing wattle trees led his eye to the taller gums that today were capped with the plumes of small white flowers. The white blossoms were so full of pollen that he could sense it in his nostrils and at the back of his throat as he breathed the air.

Today, he had decided he would paint from a very low angle viewpoint and place the rectangular canvas into a vertical position. This would enhance the long trunks of the trees whose branches flared out widely high overhead. But it was the mass that surrounded the trunk at its base that Douglas attacked first. He enjoyed rendering the undergrowth — it offered wonderful punctuation for his picture.

The charcoal drawing was done. Douglas always believed in properly draughting his subject before painting, otherwise he found he would be forever try-. ing to draw with his paintbrush as he applied the paint. In his student days he tried many short cuts as the naive are apt to do, but he would inevitably begin to draw with his brush as he started laying in the body colour of the work.

The smell of linseed oil filled the forest, attracting bees in great numbers. Douglas didn't mind the bees, it was the wasps he didn't care for. He'd been stung only once by a bee while painting in the bush, but wasps were another matter. They were territorial, aggressive and attacked without provocation. He'd been stung on at least seven occasions by wasps; once two wasps attacked him at the same time. Painful stings; he knew no remedy for them other than to remove the long barb from the skin, dab it with whisky or turpentine, and suffer.

Douglas felt good in his work. He revelled in the challenge of the task. He had the feeling of winning; he had good control of *this* canvas. The whole area was quickly covered and he settled into the finer applications that come only with experience and an artist's eye — he would render now for the keen scrutiny of connoisseurs or fellow artists. The uninitiated viewer would quickly dismiss this picture — Douglas, with his fine finishing techniques, offered the enthusiasts who viewed for longer periods their just rewards.

The first picture took him only three hours to complete. He would eat lunch, then take a walk and wait for the low-angle afternoon light before starting the next canvas, he thought. This time he planned a smaller, more intimate picture with the undergrowth filling the entire frame.

Douglas' thoughts went back to his student landscape painting days in England. The lush green countryside of the Lake District in the north country — Wordsworth's England. It still filled him with inspiration. One summer he went to sketch the random stone buildings in the villages of the area. He found Wordsworth's first tiny home, Dove Cottage, at Grasmere and sketched it many times. He learned that Wordsworth, a great walker, had gone on foot as far as Morecombe Bay, so he too made the long trek, sketching as he went. Although he hated attracting the curiosity of onlookers he would sit and sketch where he saw interesting compositions. At least English people were polite enough not to interrupt him, unlike the French and Italians. He remembered one day in Grasmere when as many as twenty people quietly observed him as he sketched. A well-dressed lady had offered him five pounds for the finished sketch. He refused, preferred to keep it to use as a reference for a large painting that he had, in fact, completed a few years later.

Wordsworth had inspired many English painters with his no-nonsense lyrics. Almost singlehandedly, he enticed Englishmen back to nature, to the outdoors, to enjoy and feast on the beauty of their landscapes. Before him, Douglas thought, Shelley and Byron had morosely intellectualised their way onto the bookshelves of the pseudo-learned, city-dwelling masses. Douglas often recited to himself the beginning of a poem Wordsworth wrote to his sister, begging her to go for a walk with him to rejoice in the spectacle of a crisp spring morning:

> *It is the first mild day of March:*
> *Each minute sweeter than before,*
> *The redbreast sings from the tall larch*
> *That stands beside our door.*
> *There is a blessing in the air,*
> *Which seems a sense of joy to yield*
> *To the bare trees and mountains bare,*
> *And grass in the green field.*

Douglas carried two precious artworks with him on his short stroll back to his camp at the mission. How different is the landscape that confronts me now, he thought. What a brilliant find for his art was this huge, dry, evergreen, unpainted, antipodean island.

Wollumbuy hadn't wanted to tell Ginny about finding the gold nugget, just in case he was mistaken and it wasn't gold at all. As he walked on the grassy fringes of the trail to Coonabarabran he planned to ask at the bank section of the post office for assistance in selling his rock of gold.

He was conscious of the usual prying eyes of the townspeople following him as he walked directly up to the post office. He welcomed the coolness of the building after the heat of the dusty road. A clerk seated at a desk, copying account items into a ledger, got to his feet when Wollumbuy approached the counter.

"I've found some gold and I want you to buy it from me ... if that's all right?" Wollumbuy said. His heart skipped a beat, then began to race. Hearing his own voice bounce around the near-empty room made him even more nervous. He unwrapped the bark from the huge yellow nugget and placed it carefully on the counter top.

"Oh my God!" was all the clerk could say. His mouth fell open; he was mesmerised. It took him quite a while to regain his composure.

"Do you want to buy it?" Wollumbuy asked.

"Yes, we'll buy it," said the clerk. "But we'll need some details and we'll have to have it assayed. Our assayer won't be back in town until Monday — but, oh my God, have we got a bleeding beauty for him!" He laughed loudly, took the rock and placed it on a pair of scales. "Twenty-one pounds two ounces ... that's ... three hundred and thirty-eight ounces!" And the clerk repeated to himself softly, almost under his breath, *three hundred and thirty ounces.*

"How much do you think I'll get for it?" Wollumbuy asked.

"You'll be a rich man if it assays out correctly," the clerk replied, smiling.

"How much?" Wollumbuy persisted.

"Three pounds an ounce if we buy it from you. That is" — he took a pen, dipped it in the inkwell and scrawled out a calculation — "exactly ... one thousand and fourteen pounds." He looked up and continued speaking almost in a whisper. "But if I were you I'd take it to Sydney — you'll get six pounds per ounce there. I guarantee you'd get more than two thousand pounds for it!" The clerk's voice shook with excitement.

It was a hot Christmas morning. The wind gathered in velocity and pulled with it the warm dry desert air from the north-west. Gudrun had promised the choir they would have one last rehearsal before the special Christmas service. Her throat felt parched and her nostrils dry as she walked quickly to the church.

The front doors were open — her small group of hand-picked Aboriginal singers, seven girls and three boys, were setting up the choir area as she approached. She enjoyed her work on the mission; she felt important, and knew she could make a difference to the lives of the Aborigines out here. If the government of the day insisted on treating them as slaves, she could at least ensure that they were well-treated while they were at the mission.

The rehearsal went well, she thought, the group was ready for the Christmas service. As Gudrun became totally absorbed in the music, it transported her away from the mission to some ephemeral place in the centre of her psyche, a place from where her thoughts often drifted to Douglas.

A few hours later, the choir was seated, wearing gowns that Gudrun had sewn especially for the occasion. The church was full. Douglas was seated in the last pew at the back of the hall. Pastor Maresch made a grand entrance with his slow march down the aisle. Setting himself up at his pulpit with his Bible and sermon notes, he confidently began his performance.

Karl cherished his Christmas service. He made wide sweeps with his arms, overacting in a dramatic production of his own creation. He would have loved to open velvet curtains, turn up the limelight and strike up the orchestra in the pit. He was a thespian for the Lord. He really wanted the applause of the congregation, not their souls — or was it the same thing? With his performance he would take them in the palm of his hand and mould them into shape. They would resemble little wooden soldiers in a line, Christian soldiers marching to war in Calvary-cross formation. He sang loudly with more purpose; he had been rehearsing too. At the conclusion of the hymn he composed himself and proffered a long introduction to Gudrun's choir.

Gudrun left her seat and walked to the pulpit but Karl would not relinquish it. She had rehearsed the choir from this position, but he would not leave *his* stage. She stood next to him, signalling to him with her body, but he would not move. She realised she had better stand on the step below him and begin, they had waited too long already. Karl smiled; he was in control.

The choir went through their first piece nervously but then the long hours of rehearsal took over and the now familiar sounds of something much repeated gave them confidence. They performed the remaining repertoire exceptionally well. Gudrun took several bows as the congregation, including Douglas, applauded loudly. She smiled as she walked back to her seat. She knew that Karl would be furious. He could never take a bow. Her choir had given a bona fide performance. His was merely an elaborate sales presentation for God.

# TWELVE

Wollumbuy had heard nothing from the post-office clerk since he left his gold nugget in the vault for safe keeping. The clerk had filled out details of his find, his name and where he lived, and assured Wollumbuy he would send word to the mission when his gold had been correctly assayed. That was two weeks ago.

This day Wollumbuy arrived at the post office an hour before they opened the doors. He sat on the grass on the opposite side of the street in the shade of a peppercorn tree. He was a very patient man. Finally a clerk unbolted the double doors. Wollumbuy immediately got to his feet, crossed the street and went inside. There were two clerks, one much older than the other, shuffling papers and opening drawers, preparing for a busy day's work. Wollumbuy walked directly up to the counter.

"I was in here ... a couple of weeks ago. I had some gold, I was selling it to the other fella who works here. The tall one, he wrote something down on some paper ... then he took my gold. He put it in your safe, over there." Wollumbuy pointed. "He said some assay-fella would be soon coming ... and he would let me know ... when it was all over, you know." He paused. "Can you pay me my money?" Finally he stumbled out his request.

"Just a moment, I'll see what I can find out," the young clerk said.

He went over to the desk of the older, more senior man. They whispered out of Wollumbuy's earshot; both appeared to show great concern. The younger one became more agitated the longer the conversation went on. Finally the older man came over to Wollumbuy.

"The clerk you spoke to before, Mr Sorenson, has left his employment and returned to live in England," he said. Then he paused, took a deep breath and sighed. "I'm sorry to have to tell you that we have no record of any gold transaction here."

Slowly Wollumbuy felt his whole body fill with rage. "Don't tell me that! He took my gold and put it in there." He pointed to the safe again.

"You may come and look in the safe if you wish but I'm telling you there is no gold here," said the older clerk.

"He's taken my gold with him, hasn't he?" Wollumbuy demanded.

"I can't say for sure," the clerk replied cautiously, "but it does sound as though that is what may have happened. If I were you I would go to the police station and swear out a complaint. They may be able to trace him or trace the gold — I don't know. They may be able to do something. We are powerless to help you, I'm afraid." The clerk shrugged his shoulders.

Wollumbuy stormed out of the post office and walked directly to the police station. There was some activity on the front steps: several Aboriginal men were being led into the station with chains on their necks and ankles. Wollumbuy changed his attitude immediately when he saw the chained men. He felt his spine go cold as he stopped and waited until they were well inside the building, then he slowly walked to the door and looked in. He could see the fat Sergeant yelling at the men as he took charge of them and led them away to the cells. A few minutes later he returned to his desk. Wollumbuy waited thirty seconds, then took a big breath and walked quickly through the door.

"I've come about someone who stole my gold," he said loudly as he walked up to the front desk.

Sergeant Thompson stared at him in disbelief. "Someone stole your gold?" he asked sarcastically.

Wollumbuy knew it was a mistake. The Sergeant came from behind his desk, walked right up to Wollumbuy and pushed his face nose-to-nose with him. "What gold could you own? Blacks can't own any-thing, blacks can't stake claims, especially mining claims. So no one could steal gold from *you*, could they?" The big Sergeant spoke louder as he went on. "You're one of the mission blacks, aren't you?"

"Yes ... that's right," Wollumbuy said.

"Well, get out of here unless you want to be dragged back onto your mission in chains."

Wollumbuy couldn't speak, he was so furious. Angrily he left the police station and went off down the main street. As he walked slowly along the road out of town, several crazy ideas ran through his head. He would kill the Sergeant; he would burn down the post office; no, he would steal all the money in the post office and then burn it down. When he got to the bridge over the slow-moving brown river he walked to the side and sat in the shade of a tree. It was an hour before he revived himself from his catatonic stupor. He would act on none of his ideas if he wanted to stay alive, he thought. He looked a pathetic figure as he slowly walked back to the mission.

Several miles from town Wollumbuy heard the sound of hooves pounding the earth. He turned to see the Sergeant and two black trackers at full gallop coming his way. The Sergeant almost ran him down.

"Wait up you, I want to have a word with you," Sergeant Thompson said.

Wollumbuy was nervous; he knew he was in trouble. "What's wrong? What have I done?" he asked.

"I'm not sure yet. Nothing, I hope. — Get hold of him. Put him down," he called to his black trackers. They jumped from their horses and took hold of Wollumbuy's arms, forcing him to the ground facedown. The Sergeant came over, placed his foot square on the small of his back and pushed. "I just want you to answer one question," he said as he put more pressure on Wollumbuy's spine. "Where did you get the gold?"

"I found it," Wollumbuy answered quickly, hoping to ease the pain in his neck.

"Where … exactly … where did you find it?" Sergeant Thompson asked as he transferred more weight to Wollumbuy's back.

"Ohhh … on the river bank … near town … beside the bridge. Right beside the bridge," Wollumbuy said.

"You had better be telling me the truth," the Sergeant said through his teeth. He kicked Wollumbuy hard on the back of the head, then called to his men to let him go. They mounted their horses and galloped away as quickly as they had come.

Wollumbuy felt blood running down the back of his neck; he knew his head was cut open. He reached for some grass and pushed it on his wound. He lay there for some time before he could muster enough strength to move.

A few days later, Ginny took Wollumbuy to talk to Gudrun. She had no one else to support her in her effort to convince Wollumbuy to stay on the mission. He said he feared for the safety of his family and their future.

"It's gone bad here now," he told Gudrun. "I can't see any reason for staying. I don't want to die here, this is not my father's country. I like to know that if I want to go somewhere, I can. But now they are bringing Kooris onto the mission in chains. They want us to stay here, like prisoners."

"What about your garden, Wollumbuy? You promised the Pastor you would stay for thirty years." Gudrun offered the garden as an incentive to stay.

"I love my garden. I love watching it become food for everyone but I feel locked in here now," Wollumbuy answered.

Ginny quietly added: "I'm expecting another baby."

Gudrun sat down with both of them on the grass in front of the house. Together they went over all the options. Ginny didn't reveal her greatest fear: that her baby might be half-white. For more than an hour the three of them thrashed it out, pursued all conceivable alternatives, at the end of which Gudrun could only agree with Wollumbuy. She said that if she herself were given the choice of staying here as a prisoner, she would take the chance and run for freedom.

Wollumbuy smiled. Over the next few days they would quietly prepare to leave the mission. Wollumbuy thought the best idea would be to go at sunset and walk through the night and all the following day. They would carry the children as often as possible in order to keep moving. That way they would soon be out of range of the Coona-barabran police and halfway to Ginny's homelands in Gunnedah.

Karl woke Douglas from a deep sleep. "Come, have breakfast with us," he said softly.

As they sat around the table all three tried to main-tain polite discussion. Karl was privately pleased to hear that Douglas would be leaving. He was also pleased to have forty extra blacks on his mission. He had never imagined the new laws would reap such rapid results. With the simple breakfast finished, the three adjourned to the porch for more coffee. The forced social interac-tion was a struggle for each of them.

"I have decided to leave today," Douglas told them suddenly.

Gudrun was visibly jarred by this shock announce-ment. Karl looked at her quickly, then back at Douglas. Douglas' gaze never left Gudrun. Karl felt himself as the interloper. Making a feeble excuse he went off to go to the church, leaving Gudrun and Douglas alone.

Gudrun sprang to her feet and almost ran inside. She wept uncontrollably as she stood at the kitchen sink washing the breakfast dishes. Douglas told her he would leave for Sydney immediately, and return to London as soon as he could book passage on a ship. Gudrun thought she had better regain control of herself before Karl came back. She told herself that she must approach her marriage with renewed enthusiasm and try to forget Douglas. Maybe she would give in to Karl's wishes and try for a baby.

"I will write," Douglas broke in on her thoughts — "and you must write back."

"Why?" Gudrun turned to face him, tears streaming down her cheeks. "We have no future together. Our time has gone. We are on totally different paths heading in opposite directions."

"Not necessarily." Douglas walked over to her, put his arms around her and pulled her to his chest.

"Don't say it, please don't be silly," Gudrun murmured into his shoulder. "We have to be realistic." She looked up into his eyes and he kissed her. Douglas knew she was right — it was unlikely that they would ever see each other again.

He went back to his camp, packed his belongings and tied them onto his horse. He set aside one canvas. Then he went to say goodbye to Karl in the church. Gudrun watched as they came out together, shook hands, and waved to each other as Douglas walked away. He picked up the canvas he had set aside — it was the first painting they had shared together at the Belougerie Spire — then walked up the slope to where Gudrun sat on the porch and presented it to her. She hugged and kissed him for all to see. Karl watched from below; upset by the scene, he walked back angrily into the refuge of the empty church.

All too quickly Douglas had disappeared — it seemed as though mere seconds had passed as Gudrun watched him vanish behind a cluster of trees on the trail heading east, alone.

Now she, too, felt alone. She tried to overcome an intense feeling of emptiness inside; it was as though a strong pang of hunger had built up in her tightly knotted stomach. She stood stunned for almost thirty minutes as her brain drifted in and out of fantasies. She sensed a silence falling over the mission as the forest took on an unusual green-brown-crimson dullness. *"What if ...,"* she said under her breath. No one heard her.

Douglas sat straight-backed in the saddle. He was in no hurry and allowed the horse to go at its own pace as they passed over the first rise. He would not look back; his feelings of longing, of guilt, were enough to cope with already. He planned to write Gudrun a letter when his thoughts were clearer, maybe after he arrived in Sydney. The pressure inside his head increased.

# THIRTEEN

Wollumbuy had finally convinced Ginny that it was time to go. He said that if they left the mission now they would be able to take in the annual Kamilaroi Bora before settling at his own clan's Moonee beach camp. She had never been to the Bora. Their clans came from all over the state to attend — some walked for three months. Ginny estimated that they would be on the trail for seven weeks. She was in good condition now, but if they left it too long when she got bigger with her new child it would be difficult for her to travel.

The Bora was held annually near the new town of Lismore. Approximately two thousand Kamilaroi and related people would attend. It always made the white authorities nervous and every year they tried to discourage it. For Ginny it would be her first really long walk. It would take them over the mountain trails of the Great Dividing Range, the tall timber country. More importantly before reaching the mountains they would pass through Ginny's ancestral land at Gunnedah. Wollumbuy agreed to stay for a long visit with Ginny's parents; he thought it fair. He knew that they would live out their days in his father's beach camp at Moonee.

The opossums scampered near their gunyah late that night. Ginny thought it was someone coming to visit. They had told no one about their plans to leave the mission except for Gudrun. All day Wollumbuy worked on a large sling made from bulrushes gathered at the creek. He planned to put both the children in it and carry them on his back. This would enable them to move quickly. Ginny had loaded their dillybag with bush food so that she would not have to stop to gather any on the way.

When they thought everyone was asleep they crept slowly out of the gunyah. Wollumbuy pulled the sling over his shoulders while Ginny lifted the children into it, one at a time. She then took her heavy dillybag onto her shoulder and they left swiftly.

A full moon lit the trail so brightly that Wollumbuy became worried they would be seen. Occasionally he climbed a tree or a ridge to look back to see if they were being tracked. Then they would walk on quickly, safe in the knowledge they weren't being followed. That night they knew that they had made good their escape from Neuberg mission.

Halfway through the next morning Ginny asked to stop for a while; she needed rest. She was feeling ill. Wollumbuy found a shaded area well away from the trail and they lay down. The children, who had slept only intermittently on Wollumbuy's back, enjoyed the respite. When Ginny felt fully refreshed she suggested getting back on the trail.

In the cool of the late afternoon, a small mob of kangaroos jumped across the trail in front of them. Wollumbuy was very tempted to take one, but prudently they walked on.

They did manage to walk for two whole days without sleep; thankfully, the dreaded trek to Gunnedah was uneventful. Time passed quickly.

Ginny's family were very glad to see her. She told them of her pregnancy and they went wild with delight. Wollumbuy's feelings were hurt because he was often left out of the proceedings but he enjoyed the way his children kept everyone amused. The baby, Charlie (Gimunga), was especially entertaining. Davy (Bintayin), his older brother was now two years old. Davy followed his father everywhere; he wanted to emulate his every step.

Sydney seemed to have flourished during the short time Douglas was in the outback. He walked in amazement through the streets of the new township. At the end of town, market gardens ran right down to the Harbour edge. When he left Sydney he remembered where experimental cornfields had been planted; that site now had acres of maize waving in the breeze. The military barracks at Hyde Park swarmed with uniformed men. The population had noticeably increased, Douglas thought. He noticed that people stopped to talk on the newly constructed footpaths without any of the polite courtesy they had often shown before. A colonial crudeness, a distinct abruptness seemed to be developing in everyone he came into contact with — except for Andrew Tweedie.

Douglas thought that he must have looked a poor, dirty wretch when he turned up on the latter's doorstep. Andrew took him in with open arms. Never had Douglas known a more generous person. Andrew had become very wealthy from his canny importation of rum, and he also benefited from the high fatality rate: he was the undertaker to refined Sydney society. He still had not married. He had designed a four-storey building at Circular Quay. The first floor had ample space for the undertaking business and a sales room for his rum transactions. The next two floors he made into his home. Rum robberies were rife, so to combat the thefts Andrew winched his rum stock to the top floor. To steal his rum, robbers would have to pass through three floors of the house.

Douglas had little trouble reserving his passage to England and stayed with Andrew for the two months before the *Porpoise* sailed. This gave him time to reflect. He watched the boats in the harbour. He watched buildings being constructed. And late one sunny afternoon he sat under the huge Moreton Bay Fig tree beside Andrew's house on the harbour and wrote a letter to Gudrun.

*Dearest Gudrun,*

*You are constantly in my thoughts.*

*Not one day goes by without my thinking of the exquisite time I spent with you. I cherish the memories of our Belougerie excursion and luckily I have the paintings to reinforce the magic of the Warrumbungles — and remind me of you.*

*Sydney has grown so fast. Things here move quickly, you really do have to have your wits about you. A day in the township can be so exhausting. I will just mention that vagabonds and villains run the streets after dark, and the bordellos stay open all night.*

*The city blacks are a shocking contrast to those at Neuberg Mission. Some are fully fitted out in the finest clothes, speak perfect English and take positions in well-established houses. In the one hundred or so years since Captain James Cook landed here they have taken to us much faster than we to them.*

*I am staying with a friend, Andrew Tweedie, a most generous host. I am sailing on the 'Porpoise' — it is an old but fast ship. It is not sailing for two months so I shall stay with Andrew and paint pictures of the harbour foreshores until then.*

*I will send you a watercolour that I did last week, it is a view of Sydney looking from my window at Andrew's house. Light rain was falling.*

*I can't say what my plans are for the future. I will write after I have been home for a spell. I shall certainly write again before leaving Sydney.*

*Yours for ever, Douglas.*

At a dinner party at Andrew's house Douglas first learned about the bourgeoisie's backlash movement to get rid of squatterdom. This was Australia's single most dramatic event since the First Fleet had sailed up the harbour. Almost thirty-four million acres of land were held under squatters' rights; they yielded less than two million pounds: the equivalent of one shilling, three and one halfpence per acre. Andrew thought it a pittance, considering that the pastoral lands in question were larger than the whole of England.

Political rallies were called. Speakers were united in voicing freedom from the grip of the big rich landholders and support for the little fellow, but the Sydney newspaper warned of *tyranny in the democratic torrent that threatened to level all barriers*. Soon the populace would *roar among the ruins, dance about the fires and revel among the pigs*.

The New South Wales government quickly passed both an Alienation Act and an Occupation Act. These were intended as a compromise to preserve the former rights of the rich while granting new rights to the would-be rich. The government did this to *keep faith with the past while offering justice to the future*.

The Neuberg mail was collected from the post office by one of the young mission boys. He voluntarily took it upon himself to walk to Coonabarabran twice a week as a service to his community. This afternoon Karl took the mail sack from him at the door of his house and brought it to the dining table where Gudrun sat mending a shirt. Karl began sorting through the parcels and letters. He found the letter that Douglas had sent to Gudrun, looked it over front and back and reluctantly handed it to his wife. She felt weak and almost fainted as she took the letter. She got up and walked slowly into the bedroom for privacy.

Her eyes welled with tears, making reading difficult. She ran her fingers over the beautifully scripted words on the page. She smiled when she finished it, then re-read it. Karl walked in and took her by the hand. She looked up; he kissed her lightly on the forehead. His breathing became deep, his kissing rougher.

"Not now … Karl!" she said, pushing at his chest. He grabbed at the front of her dress and pulled it apart with his strong hands. She pushed at him again. He forced his head onto her neck and bit her, then buried his head between her breasts. He pulled her left breast from beneath the torn fabric of her frock and sucked hard on the nipple.

"No…" Her voice became muffled as he took her chin and forced his mouth onto hers, blocking out her protests. Finally she gave in to his lust. She lay still as he completed tearing all the clothing from her body. His eyes were ferocious as he looked up and down her nakedness.

"My beautiful whore," he said as he took a handful of her hair, roughly pulled her head back and slapped her sharply across the face. He would punish her for the lustful thoughts he was sure she harboured for the Englishman.

Gudrun could see his hard erect penis pushing at the front of his trousers. He undressed quickly and forced himself between her thighs. "Whore, you love it … don't you?" he said breathlessly as he slapped her again with the back of his hand. He thrust at her violently, pushing her into the soft mattress, pounding his pelvis hard against hers. "Tell me you love it?" he gasped.

Gudrun groaned softly.

"Tell me!" he insisted and hit her again.

"I love it! I love it! I love it!" Gudrun screamed, and burst into tears. She knew it was useless to resist him.

He exploded in an intense orgasm. Gudrun heard him mutter something under his breath; it had a metre to it, like a rhyme or a prayer. He lay on top of her, exhausted, and held her tightly. After a while his breathing became heavy again and she could feel his passion swelling once more. She could taste blood from a long split inside her lip. Tears rolled down her cheeks and soaked into the pillow. Slowly, Karl ran his hand over her lower stomach and onto her pubis. His fingers caressed the soft hair between her legs then he pushed them inside her, hard. He continued pushing them in and out of her. She groaned as the pain grew worse. He rolled onto one elbow and positioned himself on top of her again.

Coonabarabran had had no rain for weeks. The undergrowth was dry tinder that crunched underfoot. The gum trees were shedding larger, drier branches as they strove for survival. Leaves hung downwards, burned by the intense heat of the sun. The creeks had dried up; only the occasional pool remained. On the horizon, high in the ionosphere, dark grey anvil-like clouds were forming in the after-noon sky.

The storm arrived with little warning. The wind swirled and gained in velocity causing the trees to bend and sway. Lightning sparkled against the black clouds, thunder crackled and boomed. Overhead a mighty thunderclap pushed masses of air ahead of its powerful sound. A big red kangaroo was startled into a frenzied run for its life. Other kangaroos joined the charge through the scrub; drawn together, they followed the leader over the well-wooded highlands.

The few koalas in this region scampered down from the trees and sheltered among rocks, caves and crevices. Goannas and snakes found their previous nests dug deep into the earth, lest they be consumed by the monster overhead. There would be some casualties today. Nature culled what man did not.

Another massive bolt of lightning struck a tall tree near the Coonabarabran bridge as thunder cracked out its death knell. It splintered, smouldered, and as one side fell it caught fire. Then the whole tree exploded. It looked like a gigantic Chinese firecracker. Embers flew everywhere, dry undergrowth fused in a bright blaze. Loud hissing sounds and explosions like gunpowder rang out through the Coonabarabran township as other trees were consumed by the inferno. Nature had put the small township under siege. Within minutes several hundred acres were engulfed in a windswept blaze. Flames were catapulted high into the sky by gases released from burning gum trees. Whole tree trunks exploded from the intense heat. The blaze created a vacuum and oxygen-rich air rushed to fill the void. The fire had opened up on a two mile wide front that swept along the valleys and gullies in the foothills of the Warrumbungle mountains. Everything ahead of it spontaneously combusted as the wind steered it over the dry land. It took on the appearance of an organic fire animal, dancing its way across the countryside. The fire headed west, away from the mission.

At Coonabarabran only Ruby and Bobby were left in the streets. All the townspeople and nearby home-steaders had mustered at the police station. Desperate, Bobby and Ruby reluctantly joined the predominantly white group. A bucket brigade was quickly established to douse down the roof of the stone-built police station as women and children were ushered inside. One by one the pine cottages, the hotel, the post office and the general store burst into flames. Embers rained down on each building in turn as the main body of the fire got nearer. The blacksmith's building and stables next door to the police station erupted like a volcano. The horses' screams were ear-piercing. All the fire fighters ran back inside the police station to take refuge, perhaps to die with their women and children.

Sergeant Thompson kept talking to the frightened group as they sat on the floor of the main lobby and offices, sweltering from the intense heat of the raging fire that surrounded them. Several buckets of water were passed among the group and they all doused themselves in an effort to cool off as the temperature rose higher, though the water was no longer cool. Seven blacks, including Bobby and Ruby, had gathered at the end of the long corridor that led to the cells, as far away from the white people as possible. The water buckets were not offered to them.

Within minutes the fire centre had passed. The temperature dropped and the men came out of their refuge to assess the damage. The police station, the symbol of law and order, had survived. Another bucket brigade was formed as the men tried to save the nearby burning buildings.

Then, as if God had personally intervened, heavy raindrops started to fall amid cheers from the near-delirious people. Sheets of water blew over the fire-torn landscape, causing huge billows of steam and smoke to rise as the water doused the hot spots. Heavy hail forced the temperature to drop even lower: a chill filled the air. The ground turned white from the smooth round ice particles from the sky. The freshness was intoxicating to breathe. The wind carried the rain, followed by the hail, along the same path that it had taken the fire only moments before.

The following morning, blackened trees, charred earth and rocks created a frightening sight. The landscape had taken on a sinister appearance. Animal carcasses dotted the black open spaces.

The Kamilaroi people in the region had been building their gunyahs on higher ground for weeks, expecting that somewhere among their people a *cleverman* would perform his rain ceremony, rain would pour down and a flood would probably result. Now it rained without ceasing for two weeks. The Castlereagh river burst its banks for a week and ran a banker for a further three weeks after that.

The *Porpoise* was ready to set sail. Douglas packed his things. He wanted to travel light, taking only one trunk and fifteen of his paintings safely secured in a packing case. He left Andrew a painting of the Warrumbungles for his generosity and warm friendship. He wrote Gudrun another brief letter to tell her he was leaving Sydney — he still thought of her constantly. Two weeks later he sailed past the mounted cannons of Fort Denison and out through the massive headlands, the gateway to the swelling sea. Douglas felt a sharp tinge of longing deep inside as he watched the land mass shrink away beyond the stern of the *Porpoise*. He

thought of Gudrun, Mar-weel, the Warrumbungles …
But mostly he thought of Gudrun.

The sixty-five day journey via Cape Horn had its
share of excitement. Douglas found the rough seas
exhilarating even when the forward mast came down. It
was holding a small storm sheet when it crashed to the
deck. The ship floated aimlessly while another storm
sheet was flown from the centre mast and repairs were
undertaken by the ship's carpenters.

As the English coast drew near they passed more
and more ships. A huge warship with an iron hull came
by, spewing black smoke from tall chimneys. Douglas
had never seen a steam warship before. The northern
hemisphere autumn air was bracing as it filled the sails
and powered the huge ship to port. The cry went up,
"Land ho!" Douglas Langton was home at last.

The mission gardens were filled with Aboriginal
workers. Karl had planned his work force very carefully: the crop must be harvested in one day. He
was disappointed that he had lost Wollumbuy, but at
last count there were thirty-three women and
eleven men in the fields. The previous week he
had organised a work team to fell gum trees and
hand-mill them into boards to make crates for the
produce. Four days later he had seventy-two crates,
which was all the large cart could reasonably hold. He
organised the workers into four crews. One gathered
the vegetables, a second brought them to the edge
of the field where another group packed them
in crates. The fourth crew carefully stacked them onto
the cart.

The sun set as the last crates were being stacked. Ropes were tossed over the top of the load, then tied and secured for the long six-day journey to Sydney. They expected to lose some of the produce on the trip; some would be damaged, some would spoil, but overall Karl was optimistic that the majority of the consignment would arrive in good condition.

The following day he awoke late from a deep sleep. He rubbed his eyes and looked out of the window. It was overcast and cool; a sprinkle of rain was falling. He bounded out of bed without disturbing Gudrun and got dressed. He did not want to lose a minute. He packed a suitcase and stowed it with the sleeping and camping gear he had loaded onto the cart the previous night. Ten minutes later he hitched the horses into the rig, climbed on board and went out through the mission gates. He did not look back. He did not see Gudrun, a blanket wrapped about her, watching from the veranda.

# FOURTEEN

Many corroborees were performed before Wollumbuy decided it was time to leave Ginny's family at Gunnedah for the annual coastal Bora. They had been at Gunnedah six weeks. The morning air was cool; it was mid-May and summer was well past. They would wear their possum skins because the mountain passes would be cold even now. The farewells were tearful but swift. At the top of the rise above the river, Ginny paused briefly. She wanted to look back over her ancestral valley one more time — she was sure it was for the last time. For the next several hours tears ran uncontrollably down her face as she walked.

For three days they travelled, seeing no one, when suddenly in a clearing, Wollumbuy spotted a group of Aborigines. He dropped the load he carried and gave instructions for the family to sit and wait. He hurried to join the all-male group, who were half-jogging at hunting pace. Ginny couldn't hear them talking from where she sat but arms were being thrown about in excited gestures during the discussion. Wollumbuy waved to the group as they departed, then rejoined his family.

"What did they say?" Ginny asked.

Wollumbuy's answer was short. "Trouble!"

Ginny reached out and took his arm. "What is it?"

"Some white men are out killing blacks. They say we are hunting the cattle stock. They also say we are killing their men and raping their women."

Ginny stared at Wollumbuy in disbelief.

He shrugged. "Don't look at me like that, that's what they told me," he said. "That mob back there are scared … on the run. They think it would be safe for us to go through Bingarra and follow the creeks to Nullamanna if we want to get to the coast."

Ginny picked Charlie up and held him close. Wollumbuy grabbed Davy and put him on his shoulders, then picked up his swag. Ginny watched Wollumbuy reach for his talisman. They walked quickly and with more purpose now. The children sensed the tension and became quiet.

In the days that followed the whole family fell into a depressed state. To avoid meeting white men who used the trails by day, they travelled mostly at first light in the early mornings and under cover of the early night. They met up with three other black groups travelling south and on only one occasion did they see white men. That was on a cold morning. Wollumbuy turned his head quickly, hushed the children and leapt to his feet. Grabbing several spears he went over the rise to investigate. In the distance he saw three well-armed men herding cattle. He went back to his family and they immediately concealed themselves amongst a cluster of nearby rocks and watched as the men drove their cattle along the valley below.

It was not until the herd had long passed and were over the far hill that Wollumbuy thought it safe to move on.

It was a cold day in early June when the family met up with a large group of the Guyambal tribe. The group of forty were moving south from their traditional homelands. Wollumbuy was well-travelled, Ginny thought proudly, as he displayed social skills she never knew he possessed. He overcame the many variations in their languages and by the end of the day they had made several new friends. They decided to stay for a short while in the relative safety of the group.

Far away to the south, Karl struggled with the two-horse team as he wheeled the loaded cart around a sharp curve in the western road. The well-travelled road was cut out of the side of a hill, below the flourishing township of Parramatta nestled in the valley. Karl planned to make it to Sydney by nightfall. The following morning he would unload his precious produce.

The Guyambal were renowned as stockmen and were often hired on the cattle and sheep stations around this area. They had developed a mutual trust with the station managers and owners. Some of their women entered into permanent relationships with the white men and bore their children.

The Guyambal camp was on the huge Myall Creek station. The Kooris seemed to get on very well with the station manager, William Hobbs. Hobbs was assigned two convicts, Anderson and Kilmeister, both of whom had been transported for life to Australia. George Anderson, a hutkeeper whose hut was very near the Aboriginal camp, had been living for five months in the bush and had taken up with one of the young Guyambal women, Impeta. Charles

Kilmeister, a stockman, was his working partner in this section of the property. Kilmeister had lived in this area for many years.

Ginny overheard *Daddy*, the white-haired elder of the Guyambal, send some children to invite the white men, Anderson and Kilmeister, to a dancing and singing festival planned for that evening. Huge bonfires were lit as the sun set behind the high plateau tops.

The songs came first; Ginny thought they were brilliant. The dancing followed, and the white men joined in as the chanting and music invaded their spirit. Everyone was bathed in soft firelight. The movement of the dancers and the expressive songs enabled all those present to become totally absorbed by the music and dance. Some took on another personae, willingly losing their individuality to join the long expressive line of human organic mass. A few were transported, trance-like, out of their bodies.

Masterton kept an office near the Sydney markets. It was a small, dirty, windowless room in the corner of a warehouse full of crated vegetables. He had agreed to meet Karl whenever he could manage to come to Sydney with his produce, but at seven-thirty this morning he seemed surprised to see him. Nevertheless he shook his hand and made him welcome. He offered Karl sweet tea and scones, his usual ritual at the beginning of his work day. A little later, Masterton assigned three of his workers to unload the mission produce and gladly paid Karl the first instalment of their agreed contract, whereupon Karl departed. For a while he walked around the bustling quay, marvelling at

Sydney's rapid growth. But he decided not to stay in the city, choosing instead to begin his homeward journey straight away and stop at an inn at Parramatta. The following day he reached the foothills of the Great Dividing Range.

Fog lay for long periods in the high mountain valleys. Karl hated the frustration of not being able to see about him when he travelled. If it got much worse, he thought, he would have to climb down to lead the horses along the road. He recalled some very sharp curves on this mountain plateau road. He remembered how he had enjoyed the views as he looked down some of the deep, well-treed ravines. Two hours later the low cloud was burned off by the heat of the sun as it climbed higher in the sky. Travelling became less stressful.

Karl knew when he was over the mountains — he could taste the dryness in the air. After ten uneventful days on the road, he looked forward to reaching home. He was tired of camping out under the cart and swallowing the red dust the horses kicked loose from the road surface as they travelled. Six hundred miles of bad roads and controlling two horses had taken its toll. Karl was tired.

The horses walked slowly, out of step, over the last rise to the mission. There it was: first Karl's house came into view, then the church and the schoolhouse. His muscles ached, his shoulders were locked in pain from days of constantly reining in the horses. With the journey almost at its end, the aches and pains seemed to get worse, Karl thought. Only two hundred yards to the gate, but he doubted that he would make it that far, the pain was so great. The cart would drop another wheel, one of the horses another shoe.

The mission dogs yapped their welcome and the blacks came running to the gate, children and adults alike. Gudrun walked onto the porch and looked out. Karl's whole body warmed. Proudly he straightened his back and smiled.

Ginny awakened next morning, the ninth day of June, to the fearsome sounds of thunderous hooves pounding the earth near her camp. There were loud screams and shouts. She peered out of the gunyah to find the camp surrounded by ten heavily-armed white men on horseback, whooping and yelping as they terrorised the camp with their antics. Wollumbuy came out of his hut and stood beside Ginny, then they both swept the children up in their arms and ran for the safety of Anderson's hut. They were followed by the rest of the Guyambal people at the camp. The men galloped the horses around them as they ran.

Anderson and Kilmeister came running out of their hut, disturbed by the frenzied horseback charge of the rough-looking men. All the Aboriginal people ran into the hut, fearing for their lives. Kilmeister knew some of the horsemen: he walked over to them and offered them a friendly greeting. Anderson was less friendly; he was very suspicious. The terrorists displayed an arsenal of swords, pistols and muskets.

From inside the hut, Aboriginal voices pleaded to their friend Kilmeister to help them. Kilmeister, who had danced and sung with them the previous night, did nothing. He feared for his own life before this vigilante mob. He suspected they were killers and he was afraid to stand in their way.

The men in the posse were not sure about Anderson. Kilmeister did most of the talking. Anderson said very little, but he could not conceal his distrust of this wild bunch. Anderson was sent to get some milk for the group. When he returned he found the men had herded the Guyambal people from the hut and had them roped together in one long line. They were being led away. The children were not tied, they were in howling panic as they trailed their crying, distressed parents.

Anderson would have no part of this. He had a real emotional commitment to the Guyambal people and he loved his woman, Impeta. Luckily she was visiting relatives some distance away. The posse left him a woman as a gesture to appease him.

Kilmeister had a decision to make. It didn't take him long. He ran inside the hut, picked up his sword and musket, saddled a horse and joined the mob.

Ginny held Charlie tightly to her bosom as she was herded away. Davy had become separated from Wollumbuy when he was hit over the head with a rifle butt in a scuffle with one of the men. Ginny looked back as they were roughly pushed along; she was in time to see Anderson usher Davy safely inside his hut. The little boy was clutching his head. Tears ran down her face; she began sobbing uncontrollably.

About two miles from the hut they were herded into a newly constructed stockyard. *Daddy*, the tribal elder, crying unashamedly, came forward to ask what was the matter, what had they done wrong. He was knocked to the ground and two shots rang out. One of the shots hit a young man standing next to him: he fell with a gaping wound in the side of his head. For the next few minutes there was great confusion as the Aboriginal people were tied in a tight group in the centre of the yard. There was loud wailing and desperate pleading from the men, women and children.

Ginny held her husband and her baby tightly as the white men put down their pistols and rifles and drew their swords. Two from the white mob moved cautiously closer. They began taunting the people on the perimeter of the roped-off circle. Jabbing at them with long-bladed swords. As the jabs found their mark blood started to spray. Then they began wielding and flaying the sharp metal weapons at the dark-skinned limbs of the trapped people, who held their arms high to protect themselves from the wide sweeping blows. Panic began to transmit itself through the mass of black bodies. Men, women and children broke into involuntary fearful screams as the rest of the white men began slicing and stabbing at random. Blood sprayed everywhere. The horror pitch of the death screams was ear-piercing. Panic-stricken children, their eyes tightly closed, clung in desperation to their parents, some of whom were already dead. Deep pools of blood caused people to lose their footing; many slipped and fell. Limbs were strewn all over the blood-soaked yard.

"You said all of the bastards, didn't ya!" Kilmeister shouted loudly as he took one of the younger children aside. The three-year-old girl was half-unconscious with the shock of having just seen her mother hacked to death, but she kicked and cried as she was thrown to the ground. Kilmeister pulled her head back and with one blow of his sword decapitated her head from her little body. Blood pulsed from the neck as the body fell to the ground. He held her head by the hair. Her eyes were still open and her mouth gaped wide. He raised it overhead and yelled as he swung it high and far. After this each of the children was systematically taken aside. Their heads were decapitated from their small bodies and thrown well out of the yard in frenzied, bloody gestures of triumph.

Ginny looked in disbelief at Kilmeister, who last evening had enjoyed Guyambal hospitality. He came over to her, muttered something, then pulled his sword swiftly down. She felt the blade hit the side of her head and slide along the bone of her skull, leaving a massive gash at the base of her neck. She fell to the ground, and as she lay, bleeding heavily, she saw Wollumbuy swinging his fists defiantly at two men who rushed at him together. She wanted to get up and fight but her limbs would not respond. She watched Wollumbuy as he managed to capture one of the men in the rope. He pulled it tight around his neck, but in doing so he became an easy target for the other man, who swiftly wielded his sword, severing Wollumbuy's left arm at the elbow. She then saw her husband stabbed in the chest many times with a dagger before he fell heavily to the ground next to her. Blood pulsed from his gaping wounds and she saw his spirit leave his body. Charlie was easily pulled from her grasp by one of the men and put over the yard fence. Ginny did not see one of the men remove his head in a single blow of his sword. She did not see the man pick up the head and throw it well away from the corral as he screamed out his crazed battle cry. Ginny's eyes rolled skyward as she lay there, struggling not to retreat into the tunnel that was forming before her eyes. Suddenly, she rushed upwards into that tunnel and everything went white, then turned light-green, then blue before it slowly faded to black.

After twenty minutes, the hysterical screaming had stopped. What remained was a horrible, macabre scene. The yard was covered with the torsos of men, women and children whose arms, legs and heads had been dismembered. Gallons of blood spilled down into the creek, turning the surface red as it flowed downstream. The children's heads had been flung far afield. The white men, their veins coursing with adrenalin, mounted their horses and rode away from the bloody scene still yelping and yahooing their murderous battle cries.

No one was quite certain how the bush telegraph worked, but in a matter of days news of the Myall Creek massacre had travelled hundreds of miles. When Hobbs, the station manager, heard of it he immediately saddled his horse and rode overnight to reach the Aboriginal campsite. He questioned Anderson who told him nothing, fearing for his own life. Kilmeister was nowhere to be seen. At first Hobbs could not find anything unusual, but he knew something had happened. All the Guyambal clothing, cooking implements, stores, fishing nets and numerous trinkets were still there but the people had gone: disappeared.

That same afternoon, Kilmeister rode back to the station hut from a week-long killing spree on the

MacIntyre River. Hobbs questioned him as to why he had left the hut when, as assigned convict labour, he was under strict instructions to stay put and mind the cattle run. Kilmeister calmly replied that he was looking for stray cattle. Hobbs was certain he was lying. He told him he knew about the murdered Aborigines.

It was at that precise moment that an Aborigine lucky enough to escape the killings — he had been working out of the area for a few days — came up to the hut and agreed to take Hobbs to the stockyard to view the ghastly scene of the massacre.

Hobbs could not believe his eyes. Cast all around the yard were partly burned, dissected bodies. The vigilantes had returned in a vain attempt to burn and bury all evidence of their crime. The stench of death and decay was horrible. It became overwhelming for Hobbs; he had to leave the scene. He walked only a few yards before he began vomiting. The earth was hard to the touch, the river clay and the blood had dried solid. Still throwing up, he recognised the remains of *Daddy*, whom he had known well. His head, arms and legs all of which had been hacked from his body lay nearby. The heads of all the children, even the babies, had been cruelly severed. Hobbs began to count the dead: he gave it up as impossible after twenty-eight. As he left, the crows and hawks came back to their feast and the flies and insects buzzed in a frenzy.

Hobbs wrote to the police magistrate at Muswellbrook. An official report eventually reached Governor Gipps at Government House in Sydney. Gipps was outraged. He saw himself as the champion of British justice in the colony. He demanded a complete and thorough investigation and the immediate prosecution of those responsible.

Eventually, Anderson came forward and gave his eyewitness account to the special police task force that Governor Gipps established. Charles Kilmeister, John Russell, George Palliser, John Johnstone, Edward Foley, Charles Toulouse, James Hawkins, John Blake, Charles Lamb, James Parry and James Oates were identified and named as the eleven men responsible. They were arrested and taken to Sydney. The trial was set down for the fifteenth of November. Primarily they were charged with the murder of *Daddy*, the tribal leader.

The people of Sydney and frontiersmen throughout New South Wales were outraged. Popular opinion was that the killing of an Aborigine could not in any way be equated with the killing of a white person. News of the case reached London, where there was no surprise that a colony full of convicts would behave in such a manner.

The Chief Justice of the Supreme Court summed up the case for the jury:

> *It is clear that the most grievous offence has been committed; that the lives of nearly thirty of our fellow creatures have been sacrificed, and in order to fulfil my duty I must tell you that the life of a black is as precious and as valuable in the eye of the law, as that of the highest noble in the land.*

The jury took fifteen minutes to return a verdict of *not guilty*. The public applause in the galleries was deafening. The law of the bush had triumphed over British justice.

But Governor Gipps and British justice were not so easily put off; on 27th November, a second trial was held. Using the *same evidence*, seven of the men, including Kilmeister, were charged with the murder of an *unknown Aboriginal child*. This time the jury returned a verdict of guilty. The two conflicting verdicts could be explained thus: Australia's new white citizens could tolerate the murder of an Aboriginal man, but never of a child — even an Aboriginal child.

On the 7th December the seven convicted murderers were hanged. Before their execution the men confessed to their horrific crimes.

Governor Gipps sent a harsh message to the frontiersmen: *Don't kill Aborigines*. When it arrived in the outback, the bush telegraph read: *When you kill Aborigines, don't tell anyone!*

# FIFTEEN

When Ginny came out of her long coma she was thoroughly confused. Her body was in shock. She could not move. She raised her head and looked about but the pain in her shoulder and neck forced her to drop back onto the pillow. She didn't know where she was, but she knew she was alive and safe.

The Williamsons, a farming family, had taken her in. They had heard what had happened at Myall Creek and quickly went to offer what assistance they could. As they stood, shocked by the bloody scene before them, they noticed that incredibly, some of the victims were still alive, though savagely mutilated. Ginny was one of three survivors they took on their cart to their home twenty miles up-creek into the hills. Out of the original three, Ginny was the only one still in their care. The other two were a young woman and an old man. The woman had lost an arm and the man had taken fourteen stab wounds to his upper body. Both, nursed back to health, had left months ago to rejoin their people.

Ginny had lost so much blood they thought she would never pull through. She had also suffered an involuntary miscarriage. A marked change came over Ginny as she lay quietly in bed under the watchful eye of Mrs Williamson. She was over the critical stage. She had suffered terrible wounds, a miscarriage and deep shock from seeing her husband slain before her eyes. She had been semi-comatose for a little over six months.

The Williamsons watched as, gradually, Ginny regained her strength. She began eating and walking — just a few steps at first. She felt it was a personal achievement when she finally walked unaided out of the door to sit under the large, brown-bark gum tree that shaded the Williamson farmhouse. It was also a triumph for the Williamsons, who had managed to get Ginny to her feet after such a long bedridden period. They had become very attached to her and were reluctant to let her go a few weeks later. But Ginny had been desperate to leave as soon as she remembered how Anderson had taken her son, Davy, into his hut. Every nerve in her body ached to find her son.

The Williamsons were childless. They had left the coastal coal-mining town of Newcastle six months before to try their hand at sheep herding. Jack Williamson was a quiet man, who moved in collective energetic bursts, allowing himself short sitting spells before spinning off into another chore. Irene Williamson was the daughter of a coal miner. Her nursing skills came from taking care of mining accident victims.

Tearfully, Ginny hugged the Williamsons before setting out for Anderson's hut on Myall Creek. She did not care about the summer sun or the miles of hot, pebble-covered trail under her bare feet. She was healthy, inspired, determined to find her boy. The journey took most of the day, and at last she came in sight of Myall Creek. She sat quietly for a few minutes, reflecting on the horror that had happened here. A strong sense of panic rushed through her body. She felt like crying but she could not; she felt like screaming but she did not. Nervously she stood up and slowly made her way towards Anderson's hut. Cautiously, she walked around it, as if it contained fierce animals. There was no movement at all. Faintly, Ginny heard hooves pounding into the earth. She fell to the ground and rolled hard into a small prickly bush, concealing herself from the lone rider she could now see in the distance. Anderson came riding up to the hut alone. Once Ginny recognised him, she left her hiding-place and ran slowly towards him. He saw her, reached for his rifle, then relaxed his grip on the weapon as he vaguely remembered her. He got down slowly from his horse and walked to greet her.

"My boy, where is my boy?" Ginny's voice wavered as she spoke.

Anderson defused her distress immediately. "Don't worry ... he is all right, he's safe."

Ginny almost collapsed with relief.

"He's with my woman, Impeta, at her camp. I'll take you there," Anderson told her as he climbed down from his horse. He took her by the arm and helped her sit down in the tall dry grass. "There, take it slowly. Have some water and rest for a while."

"No, I want my boy. Then I'll rest," Ginny told him.

"Of course. Come with me, then," Anderson said, smiling. He mounted his horse and helped Ginny climb on, leaving one of his own feet out of a stirrup to allow her to get a foothold. Ginny, slim and agile, swung onto the horse's back behind Anderson. The rocking motion almost put her to sleep as she settled into the four-mile ride. She had her arms locked securely around Anderson's waist — she felt safe and warm. An hour later they came upon a large camp of Guyambal people located outside a big rocky outcrop. Twenty Aboriginal men jumped to arms quickly and came forward with a loud, ferocious challenge. Two warning spears were hurled in the air, deliberately thrown short of their target.

Immediately Ginny spotted her son. She slid down from the horse and sprinted towards the camp. When they saw Ginny one of the men called to the warriors and they lowered their spears. They also recognised Anderson as he rode closer.

Ginny ran swiftly into the centre of the camp. "Davy!" she called.

Davy didn't see his mother right away, but after a slight prompting from Impeta, he turned and ran squealing to his mother's open arms. Ginny picked him up and they hugged each other tightly. Tears rolled down Anderson's face even as he gave a tight-lipped smile. Ginny's whole body convulsed as she sobbed. She went down on her knees, still holding her son tightly.

The sun was at the horizon and had just lost its brilliance. The Guyambal campfires were lit. The mouth-watering smell of kangaroo flesh permeated the whole area. Ginny and Anderson stayed in the camp with Impeta.

Again and again, throughout the evening, Ginny thanked Impeta for taking Davy into her clan. He had lived with the Guyambal for the past six months. Later, she also had time to thank Anderson properly for his quick, thoughtful action and bravery. He told her how the eleven men had been caught, arrested and brought to trial. He went into detail about the outcome of the trials, how the murderers were eventually hanged. She did not know what punishment could be appropriate for their horrible, senseless crimes: hanging them in no way repaid their debt to her for taking the life of Wollumbuy and her dear little Charlie.

Two days quickly passed by. Ginny watched as Davy played with the children of the camp. She decided it was time to take charge of her destiny, to resume her life. Three days later she and Davy left for Gunnedah. She had decided to rejoin her family.

Though uneventful, the journey caused Ginny great distress. She lay awake at night under the cover of hastily gathered branches, crying, thinking, remembering her family as they used to be. She recalled how only a few months back they had made this trek in the other direction, filled with hope, confident about a fresh start on the coast. She remembered that Wollumbuy had often referred to it as their *final journey*. Every day as she walked with her Davy by her side, she was constantly on the alert for white men. Every night she released the tension as she silently cried herself to sleep.

Ginny felt sick to her stomach as she and Davy climbed the final rise that overlooked her family homelands. She was excited, nervous, tired. On the long walk down to the river valley, she became more distressed because now she would have to tell why she had come back home: she would have to re-live the terror of Myall Creek.

That night Ginny sat around a huge fire with her family and a large group that had gathered. They listened in silence to the incredible events as Ginny unfolded them. During the telling of her story she had to regain her composure several times. Later that night she collapsed, thoroughly exhausted, safe in the bosom of her family.

Several months went by before Ginny began to feel she could relax and join in the singing and dancing with her people. She knew she would never forget Wollumbuy or her baby. She loved thinking about them. She marvelled at how her mind had conveniently fashioned them into cherished memories.

Sir William Mathews Q.C. was unlike any wigged barrister Douglas had ever seen. He came hurrying full-stride into his law chambers from the rain-soaked streets of London. He was thirty minutes late for his appointment with Douglas Langton and his mother.

"I am sorry … running a little late," he said as he poked his weather-beaten face around the door of his room, where his clients were seated stiffly on high-backed Chippendale chairs. Sir William's large office, with its rows of musty books reminded Douglas of his father's library. As a boy, he was never allowed simply to walk into his father's library: he had to earn the right to enter each time by explaining exactly why he wanted to go in. His father's library was no place to frolic and play.

Sir William hurried along the hallway spouting a flurry of directions to his clerks: "…the Fisher file, the Pemberton papers… and send a note of regret to Lord Russell — I shan't be able to attend his luncheon on

Friday…" Then: "Good morning, Mrs Langton, Mr Langton," he greeted his clients formally as he entered his room, tilting his head at an angle. Cleverly, he modified his tone: from the moment he sat in his stuffed leather chair he became Sir William Matthews QC. Douglas and his mother shifted on their chairs expectantly.

Sir William pushed his reading glasses onto the bridge of his rather prominent nose, then untied the red silk ribbon that bound the legal papers together. There was a pause as he read to himself, then suddenly addressed his clients. "This is the document your Great Aunt, Mrs Mary Walworth, lodged with this firm." Sir William nodded to Douglas, then continued: "In the letter I sent to you in Australia I believe I informed you that you are the sole beneficiary of her estate. The law requires that we formally read the entire contents of the document, and we shall do so later. Let me begin by telling you that you have become a very wealthy man." He riffled the pages of the Will, found the section he wanted, and read out deliberately: "The Estate and Manor house of Old Bottersley, Sussex, and all that is contained therein, including your late Aunt's valuable jewellery … Eight town houses in Belgravia, three country residences near Staines, three dairy farms in Wiltshire … Other assets include stock and bonds, cash and gold worth in excess of one million pounds. Let me see … you are now the proprietor of two substantial mercantile establishments … It is estimated that together, your holdings generate several hundred thousand pounds annually." Douglas had had no idea how rich his Great Aunt was — how wealthy he now was. He was completely overwhelmed. His mother squeezed his hand.

Sir William continued. "We engaged two banks to oversee the continuation of your Great-Aunt's business affairs. As well as several mercantile managers, we also enlisted the services of a firm of accountants, several estate managers and factors." Sir William paused as he looked up. "The firm of Mathews, Dunlop and Fraser has acted for your family for one hundred and twenty years, Mr Langton: we look forward to continuing our association in the future." At this point the lawyer noticed Douglas' expression of complete shock, and he smiled at the younger man. "As I said previously, Mr Langton, you have become a very wealthy man indeed."

After the full reading of the Will was completed, Douglas bade his mother goodbye outside the chambers. He had seen little of her since he returned to England; these days he preferred her company in small doses. They seemed to have grown apart during his many years abroad. He escorted her to her carriage, and hailed his own to come forward. He had arranged to go directly to the manor house in Sussex, to take possession of his great-aunt's stately home.

Once he was alone in his carriage, Douglas fell deep into a well of fantasy, speculating about the future. It now seemed possible for him to achieve everything he wanted in life. He was aware of his responsibility for those in his employ, whoever they were, how ever many they were. He would call a meeting of his advisers and managers as soon as that could be arranged …

The carriage turned through the gates of his newly acquired estate. A long avenue of oak trees displaying their gold-and-brown miracle of autumn ran up to the great house. Seventy-three people, the full complement of house staff, were waiting patiently for his arrival, grouped on the granite steps that led to the entrance. Thomas William Jones, the butler, came forward to introduce himself, the housekeeper and the rest of the servants, a veritable army of employees. Later there would be other employees to meet, his farm factors, estate managers, the tenantry ... Douglas thought he would never remember every name, but he did in time.

The butler, Jones, was a Welshman. Douglas soon found himself confiding in him, and took his advice on almost all matters relating to the running of the house. The first two weeks went quickly. It was exciting and exhausting. He realised the only way his Aunt could have survived the never-ending schedule of household, tenantry and business affairs was to delegate them to others ... yet this was something Douglas was loath to do. He had to take strangers into his trust and allow them enough latitude to control his affairs. He arranged monthly appointments with his mercantile executives at his London company offices and required them to provide full reports of their transactions. Just two months went by before he knew he needed help. He read all the reports he had requested — but after studying them he was none the wiser. He had to admit to himself that he could not understand the businesses he now controlled. It was an uncomfortable feeling.

# SIXTEEN

Gudrun had retreated into the monotony of a daily routine. She would get out of bed at sunrise, walk the perimeter of the mission, bathe before preparing breakfast, then spend the remaining part of the morning with the mission women. She totally immersed herself in their gathering excursions. She got to know several of the women very well and in the afternoons she began writing notes about them, their food gathering and their stories. At sunset she prepared the evening meal, after which she would read for an hour before she went to bed.

Karl took great care not to upset Gudrun. The situation on the mission was becoming more volatile with each passing month. Blacks were leaving without permission and not returning. Karl thought he could not possibly be expected to police this situation. It was out of hand. Sergeant Thompson had brought twenty more chained blacks to Neuberg last week; in spite of this Karl was in no doubt the numbers were dramatically dwindling. He estimated that one hundred and fifty Aborigines lived on his mission last year. About half that number remained. He decided to take a census, after which he would prepare a roll for weekly reference.

The mission gardens had already yielded more vegetables than anticipated and the sales from excess produce were swelling the mission coffers. Karl had large cash reserves secured away. He installed a small trapdoor in the floor of the bedroom; inside he built a pine box lined with tin, his secret safety deposit box. He carried the only key to the door with him always.

Tonight Karl sat quietly as Gudrun served him dinner. She enjoyed her thoughts and was thankful to him for not interrupting them. She urgently wanted to get back to her journal after eating. She knew Karl would want to read; a new batch of books had recently arrived from Germany.

It would be a year next month since Douglas sailed for England. She hadn't allowed herself to dwell on thoughts of him. His letters arrived regularly every two months but she would not allow herself to give them much import, in case she became too upset. They often caused her to fall into a depression from which she would not recover for days after. She took his painting of the Warrumbungles down and placed it face to the wall on the bedroom floor. She was filled with guilt, despair and longing, but she knew she had to get on with her life the best way she could.

"I'll take my walk after dinner," Karl told her.

Gudrun was surprised that he would be off on his walk so early in the evening but welcomed the time she would have alone with her journal.

Karl pulled on his heavy boots and called to Gudrun not to wait up for him. He took long strides as he negotiated the familiar slopes down to the mission gates. As he headed towards Coonabarabran, his walk

took on a determined rhythm. His gait resembled a
Prussian military march. Two miles along the trail he
turned into a bush track. It was the same track that Mar-
weel had found on the return journey from the
Belougerie Spire camp. He began a steep climb over a
large rock-strewn area. At the top he lifted a dead
branch and moved it away to reveal a huge crevice. In it
lay a cache of Aboriginal artifacts. He put a small selection of them into a sack left there for that purpose, then
replaced the branch.

The high trail to Belougerie was not well known,
even to local blacks. Karl had used it before. He had
completed the journey in good time when he visited
Gudrun and Douglas at their camp near the Spire. He
had thought, when he saw Mar-weel walk by him with
his fish catch, that either the Aborigine or Gudrun had
seen him as he moved off to visit Trevor O'Neill and his
family. The high trail had provided him with ample
time to say prayers, have dinner, murder the O'Neills
as they slept, and then return without being missed
by anyone.

He had heard another family had taken possession of the O'Neill farmhouse. He intended to pay
them a visit.

Gudrun sat at Karl's desk to write in her journal. She
thought back to the food-gathering excursion this
morning with the mission women. She wrote:

*19th February, 1871*

*What respect Aboriginal people have for the
earth. All plants and creatures that provide food are*

*harvested under strict control. Hunting rules and gathering patterns are strictly observed, enabling the food to regenerate.*

*Greed is a serious crime amongst Aboriginal people. Everyone sees to it that all members of a group receive nourishment. The supply of food must be maintained from one season to the next.*

*Ruby's husband, Bobby, is the group's best hunter. His exploits are often re-enacted through song and dance. This morning Ruby told me about a kangaroo hunt Bobby went on recently. She told me how he painted his body with mud and sand, so that he could stalk the kangaroo without the animal picking up his man-scent. He walked the cliffs looking at all the known waterholes. Then he spotted a big brown rock kangaroo. He spoke to the flies as he brushed them away from his body. He asked them not to warn the kangaroo that he was there; the flies should understand that his people were very hungry. He moved slowly, setting his spear on his woomera. The kangaroo stood, drinking, very far away. Only Bobby could throw a spear that would reach him from such a distance. Bobby took three steps and let his long spear go. It flew true to its mark. He brought the kangaroo home on his back.*

*Ruby prepared the animal for cooking. She broke the two back legs, pulled out the tendons and used these to tie the legs tightly together. She threw it on a highly stacked fire to burn off all the fur then she put it on some bark, taking care not to get sand and dirt on it. She cut open the belly, took out the heart and liver and threw them on the fire so that they would have something to eat while the big animal was cooking. She dug a hole in the ground and pulled the fire into it then she filled the kangaroo's belly with hot stones that she had placed on the fire earlier. Lastly, she covered everything with paperbark and sand. She had created a deep earthen oven. The animal was cooking from the inside as well as the outside. When smoke from the bark seeped through the sand, the kangaroo was ready to eat.*

When Gudrun had finished writing she looked up from her page. She rubbed her eyes and stretched her arms high overhead, then stood up and walked into the kitchen. She could hear singing from the camp below. She went outside onto the porch to sit, watch and listen. It was early evening; a big bonfire burned furiously and around it a group of elaborately painted Aboriginal women danced and sang. Gudrun didn't understand too much about the customs of these people, but she thought this was the conclusion of a fertility ceremony for young women.

It was then that Gudrun first saw Manduk. He was totally naked as he walked into the mission proudly bearing two kangaroos on his broad shoulders. He also carried a large number of spears and woomeras. He beamed a wide smile at Gudrun as she sat on the porch. He was tall, athletic-looking and very handsome. She couldn't take her eyes off him. To her embarrassment and surprise, she felt herself becoming excited by his nakedness. She often thought how wonderful it would feel to shed her own clothes. To feel at one with nature, to feel the breezes, the sun, the rain, the bushes, the grass, the running stream against her bare flesh. Manduk's dark body, sheened with sweat, shone in the failing sunlight. Gudrun enjoyed looking at him as he walked. He showed great style and poise. She smiled to herself. She suspected his walk was something well-rehearsed.

Manduk walked directly through the heart of the mission and made himself a camp at the far end, near the market gardens. He invited those in the camps and huts nearest him to come and share his food. Later, laughter and good-natured voices filled the night air.

Several hours went by. Gudrun decided she would take a walk through the camp. As she walked near Manduk's fire she saw he had his back to her. He was telling the group a story. Suddenly, as Gudrun reached the camp, he leapt to his full height, turned and jokingly let out a loud challenge. Then, seeing the startled look on Gudrun's face, he began to laugh. Gudrun was shocked. He asked her in his broken English to sit with them. She nodded; yes, she would like to. She sat and smiled at those she knew: Ruby, Bobby, a few of the women with whom she gathered food. Manduk was a master storyteller. A talent as prized in Aboriginal society as the skill of a good hunter. The stories continued throughout the night, punctuated by much laughter. Gudrun could understand little of it, but she sat mesmerised by Manduk's deep melodic voice and dramatic gestures. She knew she was staring at him; but she could not help it.

The gathering broke up, and Gudrun walked back to the house. What an exhilarating evening she thought. She had sensed for several months now that she was being accepted into the Aboriginal community. She went to bed that evening with a fresh outlook on life.

That night a strong wind whirled through the high limbs of the gum trees at the rear of the house. The sound of a rhythmic human voice harmonised with the wind. Half-asleep, Gudrun felt her body being softly caressed by three or four men; at least one of them used feathers to heighten the sensuality that consumed her. She felt her body move in rhythm with the erotic chanting. The men's caresses fell in time with her movements. Suddenly she tossed so hard that she sat bolt upright, startled, eyes wide open. She could still hear the wind and the chanting. She went to the window and looked out. Manduk was lying naked on his back on the ground ten paces from her. He writhed as he chanted his erotic love songs. Four more men sat a farther ten paces away, chanting in alternate rhythms to Manduk and stroking the earth with feathers and leaves. Gudrun felt her heart thumping in her chest; it became difficult for her to breathe.

She stepped back from the window, let her night-dress fall to the floor and walked to the bed. She lay back naked, relaxed, and listened to the chanting as it continued. She caressed herself, letting her body surrender itself to eroticism. She moaned loudly as she experienced her first orgasm. Then slowly she drifted back to sleep.

Karl arrived silently at the side of the O'Neill farmhouse. He looked inside; a candle was burning near the window. In the dim light he could see a young woman lifting a sack of flour onto the table. There was no one else in the house. He went to the front door and knocked. The woman called through the door: "Who is it?"

"Karl Maresch. I'm your local pastor," he said cheerily.

The woman opened the door and smiled. "My husband's not here. Can I help you?"

"I only wanted to introduce myself and invite you and your husband to our church," Karl told her.

"I'm not sure. We do go to church sometimes … Come in, anyway, and wait for my husband."

Karl entered the house and seated himself at the rustic dining table.

"My name is Julia Pritchard. I'm sorry my husband's not here to meet you. He's in town … he's been there all day." The woman offered Karl a cup of tea which he gladly accepted. She went to the kitchen bench to prepare the brew.

"I do a lot of work with the Aborigines. I have some of their artifacts here. Would you like to see them?" Karl pulled some Aboriginal objects out of his bag, and began to explain the significance of some of the pieces. He took a huge nulla-nulla in his hands and stood up to demonstrate its use.

Julia turned away to attend to the tea, and as she did so Karl seized the moment. He leapt towards her and swung the club at her head, crushing her skull with one mighty blow. She crumpled to the ground.

One side of her face was a bloody pulp of bone and flesh, her left eye resting on her crushed cheekbone. Karl threw down the club, twisting Julia's face away as he rolled her over onto her back. He ripped her dress open, feverishly tearing off her undergarments. Blood was still pumping from her open head wound onto the floor. Karl's eyes were bulging from their sockets. He had a crazed expression on his face and began to salivate uncontrollably. He ran his trembling hands over Julia's firm, warm breasts, pinching her nipples tightly. He scratched and scored her lower stomach very deeply with a decorated bone implement, drawing more blood. He pushed the bone deep into her vagina. His actions became faster as lust and adrenalin pulsed through his body. He looked around the room, reached for the cup of tea and poured it slowly over her near-naked body. Then he slowly caressed her wet skin, pushing his fingers into her warm tight openings. After his excitement had peaked he got to his feet and quickly left the farmhouse.

It had all happened so swiftly. Blood still poured freely from Julia's head. It carried tiny pieces of splintered bone with it before soaking into the bare timber floor and dripping through the cracks into the soil below.

Karl's heart thumped loudly as he ran out of the front door and into the cover of darkness and the bush. When he reached the nearest thicket he stopped and massaged his groin as he waited for his excitement to subside. Soon, her husband would return home.

The next morning Gudrun watched Karl as he tended the gardens with his helpers. She saw Manduk walk up to him and offer to help. In his broken Kamilaroi, Karl told Manduk he must cover his genitals if he wanted to stay on the mission. Manduk immediately reached down, picked up a handful of mud and rubbed it over his penis. Karl broke into a fit of laughter. Gudrun contained her own laughter — she must not draw attention to herself. From that moment everyone, even Karl, accepted that Manduk would not ever wear white man's clothes.

The following day Gudrun awoke early and again walked to the gardens, passing Manduk's camp, but he was not there. Ruby, who was sitting under a tree nearby, told her that he had left suddenly last night. Gudrun confessed that she would have liked him to stay, that he had brought a much needed freshness to the mission. Ruby agreed; she knew exactly what Gudrun meant.

# SEVENTEEN

Douglas sat alone at the huge dining table. Much as he loved the old manor house, he had already arranged to move into one of his town houses in Belgravia. It would be more practical. He could conduct his business meetings in the large reception rooms.

The newly constructed, white-painted house in Chester Square, Belgravia, was five storeys high, with four tall Doric columns holding up a shallow, Grecian-styled roof over its deep porch. It matched exactly the neighbouring seven houses in the row. Douglas owned them all.

Once he was well ensconced in his Belgravia house, Douglas would rise early every day to take his habitual walk, unless the city was suffering one of its 'pea-soupers'. Mildly foggy weather and the piles of horse dung in the roads he took for granted: a million chimney stacks poured smoke into the air, and all the traffic was horse-drawn. He enjoyed strolling through the streets, he enjoyed the shops, the restaurants, the public houses, but most of all he enjoyed the people. He was never bored in London.

His two mercantile businesses were cleverly dependent on each other, while at the same time offering services to others. The Wiltshire Produce Company grew and preserved food and dabbled in the London stock market; the Oak International Shipping Company transported food, fuel and other necessities.

The nature of Wiltshire Produce was very complicated in its organisation and operation. It was run by a Scot, James MacInnes. Douglas owned three of the farms that contributed to the company's considerable output, but there were another fifteen farms, an abattoir, a fishing fleet, a canning works and numerous warehouses linked by elaborate administration and accounting systems devised by MacInnes. This company also bought and sold stock on the London exchange.

Oak International Shipping was conventional in its operation but the sheer volume of its trade was staggering. It offered overland and overseas cartage of practically anything to anywhere. The company was managed by William Magnusson. Magnusson had worked his way up through the company, starting from the warehouse floor as a boy of eighteen. He was now forty-nine. Douglas' Great-Aunt had personally promoted Magnusson to the top management position, after he had come to her with a proposal that centralised operations, increased profits and simplified voluminous accounting procedures.

Douglas scheduled his next monthly meeting with MacInnes and Magnusson at Chester Square. He was subjected to the usual well-documented presentation, as well as the verbose explanations which followed. Usually he would dismiss Magnusson quickly, then discuss the complicated Wiltshire Produce business in more detail with MacInnes.

James MacInnes was a canny man. He was from Edinburgh. His father, now retired, had been head clerk for Reynolds Shipbuilding. He had gone to great lengths to make sure there was a place for his son in the same business, and young James had joined the accounts department under his father's watchful eye. James flourished; he had no idea he would enjoy accounting procedures so much. He searched the libraries for books on business principles. He had soon read himself to loftier heights than his father had ever dreamed of: he became Controller for Reynolds Shipping, and his father's supervisor.

James MacInnes was not well liked by his subordinates. By the time he had served one year as the company Controller he implemented his first master-stroke in business, and saved the ailing company hundreds of thousands of pounds. As a by-product of the re-organisation he actually made his father redundant along with fifty other men from the work yards, most of whom had twenty or more years of service with the company.

James MacInnes was a very canny man.

"I cannot understand why you keep the business of all the different subsidiaries in one book," Douglas admitted to MacInnes when they were alone.

MacInnes smiled smugly. "Business is complicated in these times, Mr Langton. Planned growth is a natural part of good management today. What I have devised is a system that will enable Wiltshire Produce to grow and develop. Our results speak for themselves. We always show a handsome profit."

"Our results are not as good as they were," Douglas interrupted.

"What ... what do you mean?" MacInnes' composure was ruffled.

"I don't know how and I don't know why, but I can read the bottom line. Wiltshire Produce is less profitable now than it was last year, and less again than the year before. I hoped you might be able to tell me why this is so." Douglas stared at MacInnes for any indication of guilt.

"I can't explain the whole situation ... it's very complicated. I will look into profit comparisons with previous years for you and send them for your consideration." Looking flustered, MacInnes gathered his papers together.

"No," Douglas insisted. "Tell me now in simple terms why you think this situation has come about."

"I am sorry, I cannot," MacInnes said slowly. "It will take some analysis."

Both men regarded each other in mutual dislike.

"Is that all, Mr Langton?" MacInnes asked finally.

"For now, MacInnes," Douglas was fuming.

They agreed to meet the following week when MacInnes would explain the receding profits. After MacInnes left, Douglas sat at his desk in silence for an hour, then quickly got to his feet, donned his overcoat and went for a walk beside the Thames. As he walked along the river the idea came to him like a lightning bolt. He would make an attractive profit-sharing offer to Andrew Tweedie, to persuade him to come back to London and manage his businesses.

Douglas' offer reached Tweedie three months later. Andrew had no hesitation in deciding to accept it. Douglas would make him a very wealthy man. He wound up his Australian affairs and was aboard a ship bound for England within three weeks.

A red dust willy-willy spiralled across the main street of Gunnedah as Ginny, her mother and two women from her camp turned the corner at the eastern end of the town. It was very hot. The four women stopped in the welcome shade of a shop awning and sat on the wooden veranda. Some Aboriginal children played nearby, teasing a dog which was tied to a post in front of the hotel opposite. Frustrated and annoyed by the children, the dog's bark became increasingly loud.

Two men burst from the hotel, rushed the children, kicking, striking any of them within reach. One grabbed the oldest boy by the hair and began beating him with his closed fists. The others ran out of sight. Then together the two men beat the youth mercilessly as a crowd gathered and cheered from the hotel doors.

At that moment a sulky drew up and the driver leaped from his seat. He pulled one of the men away and felled the other with one blow. The stranger then stood in front of the boy beckoning the two men to come ahead. They turned and left the scene, hurling obscenities and shaking their fists at the cowering boy.

The women and Ginny remained seated at the far end of town for some time before they dared to move down the street.

Sergeant Thompson examined the scene of the farmhouse slaughter at Belougerie. The woman's body had badly decomposed during the last two weeks. She lay exactly where Karl had left her. Flies and maggots feasted on the rotting flesh and the stench finally overcame the big Sergeant. He covered his face with a handkerchief to reduce the pungent odour, came back to the woman, kneeled down and pulled the sharp bone implement from between her legs. He held it close and wiped it clean to examine the Aboriginal markings.

"*Cooee!*" The call came from the nearby scrub. The husband's body had been found by one of the policemen as he combed the perimeter of the farmhouse grounds. It too was badly decomposed, with a long hunting spear still protruding from the dead man's chest.

Thompson ordered his men to take blankets from the bed and tightly wrap the bodies in them. A large grave was dug and both bodies were slowly lowered in. The Sergeant said a short prayer and the graves were filled in. Then he gathered together all the Aboriginal artifacts and left.

News of the dreadful murders spread fast throughout the Coonabarabran region. There was talk of raising a vigilante group, a posse, to take care of the black problem. Sergeant Thompson worked quickly to regain control. His police band was increased to twelve, mostly with the inclusion of blacks from the north. The northern blacks had no allegiances with clans from this district, in fact some were traditional enemies and cherished the opportunity to use their new authority to settle some old scores.

It was not long before another chained, battered and starving group of Aboriginal men was herded onto the mission. The chains cut into their ankles and necks. Many had open sores, festered and fly-blown. Karl eagerly signed the papers which acknowledged receipt of the sorry group. Their chains were unlocked and they sat or lay on the grass, relieved that their ordeal was over.

Karl went to the group and walked amongst them, talking quietly, building trust. Gudrun watched from the porch. She felt anxious; a tightness pulled at her chest. She felt like throwing up. Slowly she walked inside and lay on the couch.

An hour later Karl walked onto the porch feeling pleased with himself. He turned to look back. "Now we are getting somewhere," he said to Gudrun in German. She made no answer. He gazed across the compound at the new arrivals. "Don't you think so?" He turned to look at her, demanding a response.

"I hate it!" Gudrun said loudly. She grabbed quickly at her mouth but the words had escaped. She got up and almost ran into the bedroom.

Darkness was falling three hours later as Karl went to the door of the bedroom and knocked softly. Gudrun stirred and rolled onto her side. Karl knocked again.

"Please go away," she said.

Karl opened the door, walked slowly to the bed and sat on the edge. "I would like you to approve of what I am doing here on the mission," he said softly. "It means a lot to me. My life's work is here. The prime reason I am alive lies here. It is only just starting to come to fruition … now."

Gudrun turned quickly. "I hate it. Can't you see what is happening? There is a war going on here. This whole country is being invaded. It is happening slowly, but make no mistake: it is an invasion and we are playing our part in it. We are custodians of a British prison camp. Yes, that is what we are."

Karl's face was drained of colour. He stood upright and quickly left the room, slamming the door as he went. Gudrun heard him fumbling and banging his way around the kitchen. He kept muttering; occasionally he would walk up to the closed door and yell through it. He stayed in this rage for more than an hour, at which point he left to take a walk.

As he strode briskly along the road to Coonabarabran, Karl vowed that he would demand Gudrun's respect and support in his mission work. He thought back to the time in Germany when he had received word that he was being considered for a mission. She had been as excited as he was. Now she had lost sight of the overall plan. They were educators; more importantly, they had won many Aboriginal converts to Christianity. He must again fill her with the enthusiasm she had once had ... or he would he get rid of her.

Gudrun could hear someone on the porch. There was a loud knock at the front door. Shuffling barefoot across the floor in the dark, she opened it. Manduk stood there, tall and naked. He carried several spears and was beautifully painted.

"I have come to take you away," he said. "You can be my woman now." He reached out and grasped her firmly by the arm.

"No, I can't ... Manduk!" She pushed at his chest. "I have to stay here." She was filled with fear, with excitement. Her pulse raced, her temples pounded with the rush of blood.

Manduk pulled her from the porch. She let herself follow. He pulled her close. He could smell her body as they walked. She could feel the power in his arms.

"I cannot go away with you. In my law it is not allowed," Gudrun said.

"I sang you my songs and you heard them. You are mine," Manduk answered as he looked down into her eyes. "You heard my songs, didn't you?" he asked.

"Yes, I heard them," Gudrun said.

"You liked them, they came into your body — is that not so?" he persisted.

"Yes," Gudrun admitted. "But I cannot go away with you."

Manduk pulled her urgently into the cover of some trees. His huge arms enfolded her. His hands ran over her breasts, her hips, her buttocks. She did not protest. The figures of the black man and the European woman melted away into the dark night as they walked deeper into the forest.

Gudrun arrived home alone at first light. She peered into the bedroom at Karl asleep in bed. Quietly she closed the door, made herself a bed on the couch, curled up and went to sleep.

Ginny rarely went to Gunnedah alone. Most days she went with other women. She felt safer with them. But this morning she needed time to herself, so she left Davy with her mother at the camp and walked the three miles to town alone. The river ran swiftly as she reached the end of her journey and began to cross the bridge.

She noticed branches floating in the strong current, indicating more land clearance upstream. A sulky came up behind her as she got halfway across. She stepped aside as it drew near.

"Want a ride?" A male voice called to her.

Startled, she turned and looked at the round, smiling face of the man seated on an old dilapidated buggy. She had seen him before — it was the same man who had intervened to save the Aboriginal child in the street brawl the month previous.

"No, thank you. I'm only going … just there." She pointed to a store on the main street as she spoke.

"Never mind. Jump on." He reached his arm down to help her climb up.

Ginny took his wrist and stepped onto the moving buggy. They both laughed as she sat down. They rode the remaining three hundred yards into Gunnedah together.

"My name is Eugene Griffin. And what are you called?" The man spoke in a broad Irish brogue.

"Ginny," she replied. His accent sounded funny. He was also dressed differently to most white men Ginny had seen. He wore a green hat with a narrow brim, baggy plaid trousers, a black waistcoat over a white shirt with no collar. His jacket lay on the seat next to him.

"I work on the Gibson property," he told her. "I ride the boundary. You know, fix the fences."

The Irishman pulled his buggy to a stop in the town centre, and as he tied his horse to a hitching rail they arranged that if they had both finished their business in an hour he would give her a ride back to her camp. The Gibson property lay three miles farther north.

Ginny bought the sack of flour she had come to town for and went to wait near the buggy for the promised ride. Two hours later Eugene Griffin emerged from the hotel opposite. She guessed that he had consumed a few beers after his shopping. He walked briskly, carrying two food sacks on his broad shoulders. He smiled when he saw Ginny waiting.

"What took you so long?" he said.

Ginny thought the joke hilarious and burst into a fit of laughter as they loaded their goods on the back of the small buggy. Eugene reined in the old chestnut mare and slowly walked her homeward over the bridge. He liked to make people laugh. His mind habitually raced round for pieces of information he could put together that would sound amusing.

He turned sideways to have a good look at Ginny. She was dressed in a cotton floral frock that hugged her body. The bodice buttons were missing so that it was open at the front, revealing her ample cleavage.

"How old are you, Ginny?"

"Nineteen."

"You speak very good English."

"I have been speaking English for many years. A lady schoolteacher lived near us when I was young. She taught me."

Ginny enjoyed talking to this white man. She felt she could trust him. She enjoyed being with him. It was as though the dark, hideous experiences that lurked in her mind had suddenly retreated. Some of her people might object to their being alone but she didn't care.

Lots of black women lived with white men, some even married them and had their children. She had seen their light-skinned children, and she knew that therein laid the fear of her people — they weren't dark enough to be called Koori, nor light enough to be called white.

Eugene talked to Ginny about Ireland for the entire journey home. He told her he was from Waterford, in the province of Munster. He told her that the sea surrounded Munster on three sides, with Waterford on the east coast. Waterford, with its deep-water harbour, had ships calling in from all over the world. He had worked on a farm — it was a rich farming area. He painted a vivid picture of how the wild Norsemen had come to Waterford over a thousand years ago. He told her he had lived on the outskirts of Waterford, in a village called Lismore, near a great castle. That was the reason he had gravitated to the new Australian town of Lismore built on the northern coast of New South Wales.

Ginny was very interested in Eugene's stories. She was putting together a puzzle in her mind, filling in pieces that would eventually give her a better view, a better overall understanding of these strange white people from far away.

She felt the chill of the early evening breeze. Eugene noticed how she braced herself against the direction of the wind. He still held memories of how cold he was in Ireland. "Here, take my jacket." He took off his short Donegal tweed coat and placed it over her shoulders. She felt his body heat trapped in the heavy weave. "I ... I'd like to see you again, Ginny, if you agree," he said tentatively. "Would your people mind?"

"No, they wouldn't mind … I suppose it would be all right." She giggled as she accepted his suggestion.

He reached over and took her by the hand. She looked down as his white hand squeezed her own dark brown one.

The trail to her camp came too quickly. The red sky shimmered on waves of low nimbus cloud overhead. To the east the darkness of night slowly pulled its veil over the day. The buggy bounced to a stop on the bumpy roadway.

"Can I drive you any closer?" Eugene asked.

"No, this is good," Ginny replied.

"When may I come to visit?"

"Whenever you like." She smiled, then added: "Next week, Saturday, in the morning like today. I'll meet you right here." She pointed at the ground on which she was standing.

"Right you are," Eugene said. "See you on Saturday then, Ginny." He let out the reins, flicked the slack lines on the horse's back and emitted the strangest yell: "Yip, yip, yip!" he called to the horse in a high-pitched tone. "Gee up, fella." He called it *fella* even though he knew it was a mare.

Ginny smiled as she watched him drive off in the failing light. She would need to do some explaining to her parents, she thought. It might not be so simple, keeping company with this handsome, jovial white man.

The camp population had grown much larger since Ginny had lived here as a girl. There were many young families with parents about her own age, products of large families who in turn had produced many children of their own. The gunyahs were strewn about the hill-side, giving the impression of a village. Many fires burned; smoke filled the canyon behind the village. Ginny loved it here. She walked up to where her mother sat under her family shade tree, scrubbing yams she had dug out of the earth that morning, and placed the heavy sack of flour beside her.

"Some flour for you, Mother." Ginny spoke in the Kamilaroi tongue.

"Thank you, daughter," her mother answered, and kept on with her chore.

# EIGHTEEN

Pastor Maresch called a special prayer meeting, and when it broke up he told as many of the mission Aborigines as he could, without being too conspicuous, that he was taking a long walk. Shortly before the meeting began he had carefully arranged some Aboriginal artifacts around the bedroom in his house while Gudrun was out visiting the mission women. One by one he placed the pieces with great care. *I am becoming expert at this*, he thought cheerfully.

Karl walked with a rhythm. He liked to sound out a metre in his head and try to keep to it. This was taught to him by his father. Karl often thought back to his strong-willed father. He had totally controlled his son as he was growing up, imposing his own defects upon him. Even now Karl still lived in fear of his father. He remembered too well the beatings and the reign of terror under which he and his mother had existed. His father would make his mother bend over the bed, lift her dress, and spank her naked buttocks with his belt until he drew blood. The beatings happened more often as he got older and they were more brutal. He beat both mother and son, as if to test how much pain they could stand. He tied Karl to a bedpost one night and beat him until he passed out from the pain. If his mother dared to interrupt she would be subjected to further violence.

Karl walked on with more determination. He could never forget the look on his father's face when, late one night, he had walked into his parents' bedroom at the wrong time. His father was in the worst rage Karl had ever seen. He had turned to look briefly in his direction, then returned to beating his wife, bent over the side of the bed and covered in blood. This was not his father, Karl thought. He did not look anything like his father. The contorted facial muscles, the salivating mouth, the wide eyes … On that one occasion he had dared to stop his father. The ensuing brawl ended with Karl being knocked unconscious.

He had known then that unless he moved away from the family home either he or his father would be killed. Just three months later he married Gudrun and the nightmare was over — at least for him. His mother stood by her husband, respecting her marriage vows: to honour, cherish and obey, Karl thought sardonically. If she left home, it was more than likely she would end up with no money, no property, no legal rights and no place in polite society.

Karl could walk twice as fast as most people. He had developed a long, unrelenting stride and a horizontal arm action. He loved to walk, it was his private time to think, to meditate, to reflect, to plan. Tonight his thoughts were of Gudrun and his plan was to be rid of her.

He broke into a sweat even though it was a cool night, but still maintained the rhythm of his stride. Finally his gait slowed as he turned into a seldom used trail that would take him high over Baraba Mountain and back behind his house at the mission by a craggy, perilous route.

The night air descended over Neuberg Mission. Smoke from the campfires rose slowly then flattened out in a horizontal stream. At Ruby's camp Gudrun was quizzing some of the women about their lifestyle. She struggled to read her notes by the firelight — the sun had set an hour previously. Ruby and two other women had small, sleeping children on their laps. Gudrun marvelled at how these women managed. What she had learned today was that the men and women worked only three hours a day, but it was a full work period, a personal duty to the clan that could not be shirked.

The women adjourned their meeting amid laughter and raised voices and dispersed quickly. Gudrun gathered her papers and placed them in the dillybag she had made for herself under Ruby's supervision. Slowly she walked the few hundred yards back to the house. She revelled in her new work — her journal. She did not know if others had recorded the world of the Australian Aborigines, but she cherished the knowledge freely passed to her by the Kamilaroi women.

The house was in darkness. Karl must be taking one of his walks, Gudrun thought — or perhaps he was caught up in his work at the church. She lit the lamp on the table near the front door and carried it to the bedroom. For some reason, strange Aboriginal artifacts were strewn all over the room.

Gudrun shrugged and set herself up at her desk to continue writing her journal.

In German she wrote:

*8th March, 1871*

*The traditional roles for men and women were clearly defined in legends of Aboriginal ancestors in the Dreamtime. Women were required to gather vegetable food by digging for yams and tubers. They gathered seeds and fruits and made unleavened bread, "nardo", from seeds. Men were required to hunt and bring home meat, usually kangaroo, wallaby, opossum, snakes or the giant goanna lizard for the family. They also fished with nets and spears. Everything was shared by the whole clan with a strict division of the catch, carefully observed. Certain parts of the animals or vegetables were allocated to certain clan relatives.*

*The whole group of clans moved camp if there was concern for the animals or bushes being in short supply. They would never take the last remaining food from the area. Plants were left to grow and animals to breed. The whole area was allowed to regenerate. To encourage regeneration they would often deliberately burn out a section of the district. This got rid of unwanted weeds and stimulated plants into extra limb growth. Fuller bushes and trees resulted, therefore more food.*

*Gudrun paused briefly to reflect, then continued once more.*

*I have found Aborigines are not an isolated surviving people with a stone-age culture. They are not*

*much different to contemporary European Cau-*
*casians, with the same human urges we have. They*
*do have a different way of living, a different per-*
*spective on life, different sets of values.*

*We draw conclusions with limited information*
*about these people. The use of stone implements,*
*for instance, should not label forever the*
*intellectual capacity of these people. Rather it*
*should tell us that they have a deep relation-*
*ship with their natural environment. These people*
*have an absence of material goods, lack complex*
*housing or community structures, they hunt*
*and gather, yet their central theme is identical to*
*our own: survival.*

*The present European invasion is yet another chal-*
*lenge for Aboriginal people, who have historically*
*demonstrated a remarkable ability to adapt and*
*survive. Perhaps this is their greatest challenge...*

Suddenly Gudrun heard a shuffling at the front
door. "Karl ... is that you?" she called loudly. She put
down her pen and went to see who or what was on the
porch. As she reached for the door it was quickly pushed
open. Manduk stood there in the dim moonlight.

Early signs of spring were visible in the green English
landscape. An abundance of colourful blooms gave evidence of the winter's end. Tall, bare elm and larch trees
renewed their branches with light green buds. There
was a cold wind blowing from the north; Andrew
Tweedie braced himself against the breeze as he alight-
ed from the train at Victoria Station.

Douglas had come to meet him. As soon as Tweedie saw him he felt reconciled to the fact that he had traded the sub-tropical Sydney climate for the early spring of England. The warmth of their friendship was enduring.

For his part, Douglas was vastly relieved that Andrew had arrived at last. He told him so. The journey to Sussex gave Douglas ample opportunity to pour out his business concerns to Andrew, who seemed to have a remarkable capacity to absorb what Douglas sourly termed *a very complex situation*. By the time they reached the Manor house, Douglas had unburdened himself of the management load and Andrew had happily taken it from him.

"Worry no longer; that is my job now, Douglas," he said as they pulled into the long driveway.

That evening Douglas had invited fifteen guests to dinner, including his mother, to extend a formal welcome to Andrew. For his part, Andrew was flattered by the way Douglas had asked for his help, and the faith his friend placed in his business acumen. The long dinner came to a close and as the gentlemen called for their brandy and cigars, the ladies welcomed the retreat to the large gallery at the front of the house, which contained many paintings by prominent artists, among them Gainsborough, Constable, Turner and, of course, Douglas Langton. Douglas' mother, an eager collector herself, gave a tour of the works for the ladies.

The men wanted to hear news from the raw new colony.

"You'll be in great demand socially," Douglas warned Andrew. "Everyone wants to know about

Australia." As he spoke that word, *Australia*, a ringing began in his ears, a long reverberating sound. He thought, *have I really been home a year?*

*Gudrun* ... suddenly he could see her long blonde hair framing her face.

He experienced a nostalgic feeling of warmth as he listened to Andrew give his account of Sydney and its shortcomings. Andrew knew little of Australia's outback; he had never been farther west than Parramatta. As he spoke, Douglas' thoughts were all of Neuberg Mission ...

The evening slowed down as guests began to leave. It had been a huge success. Andrew had not felt so stimulated for years. And Douglas' confidence in his choice of business manager was confirmed. He took care to tell Andrew just that as he retired for the night.

Hurriedly Gudrun packed a bag, took a warm wrap for her shoulders, pulled the blanket from her bed and joined Manduk on the front knoll that led to her house. She welcomed the cover the night offered as they stole away, hand in hand, through the scrub. As well as his usual spears, boomerangs and woomeras Manduk carried a small glowing ember, a stick from his previous fire. She found out later that this was his custom whenever he travelled at night, to ward off evil spirits that lurked in the dark. It also meant they could make a fire quickly when they camped.

In the dark Gudrun relied on Manduk's sureness of the bush to guide her. She felt safer, more confident with him than anyone she had known. It wasn't only his physical size and bulk that offered safety and protection. Manduk had a well-developed sense of place, of centre. He was so confident, so sure of himself and his abilities. There was an invisible aura of power surrounding him. He piloted them surely along a mountain trail. They climbed high into the foothills, pausing only once to look back when a sound startled Gudrun, causing her to gasp out loud.

"A night animal," Manduk said, and they continued on.

He had remarkable eyesight; Gudrun believed he could see in the dark almost as well as in daylight. Now he turned to face her, a concerned note in his voice. "Can you see your way?" he asked.

"Yes, I can." She was sure he had read her thoughts. Ruby had told her about *clevermen* who could do unexplained supernatural things. *Clever* children were identified at an early age and encouraged to become apprenticed to *clever* elders. Thought-reading and mental telepathy were well-known and accepted gifts amongst Kamilaroi people. Ruby had told Gudrun of a personal experience between her sister and herself, communicating through one of their arms. Whenever one needed the other they would send a signal. It seemed as though their thoughts were transmitted through the ether into the muscular nervous system of the other. It never failed them.

Manduk interrupted her thoughts, gesturing to a cave he had established for them. Gently he led her inside. Gudrun was overcome with nervous excitement as she entered the large cavern. Manduk told her to sit on her blanket, then he quickly collected dried grass and twigs to which he applied his firestick. The flames flared brightly, illuminating the entire cave.

Gudrun was delighted to discover that the walls and ceilings were covered with paintings and carvings. Large, heart-shaped faces were etched into the soft sandstone. The paintings were of faces also, large economically drawn faces with lines radiating from them. They seemed to emit some magic that invaded Gudrun's thoughts. She was completely swept away by the moment, the place and Manduk.

Karl walked slowly up to his house and peered through his bedroom window. The lamp was lit, Gudrun had left papers on her desk, the bedcovers were pulled back, but he couldn't see her anywhere. As he waited his breathing became heavy and his heart pounded in his chest at double its normal rate. He stood there, outside the house, for several hours, waiting for Gudrun to return. At last the sky turned grey: dawn had broken. Karl was exhausted. He went inside, cleared the Aboriginal artifacts away from the bedroom got into bed. He stared at the ceiling for a long time with strange thoughts torturing his mind, making sleep impossible.

Karl's world was changing. The world he grew up in was so different from the one in which he now lived. Once again he had serious doubts about his religious conviction. Several years back he had read Charles Darwin's book *On the Origin of Species*. Along with other works, it had caused Karl to question his firmly-held beliefs about the creation of the world. But after weeks of reflection he had managed to overcome his doubts. His theological training saw him through it. The Biblical story of creation was still widely accepted by all Christian churches. However, the recent publication of Darwin's *The Descent of Man* had caused him to question the uniqueness of man, the Virgin birth, the Resurrection, and the Ascension. He could no longer hold the belief that God would allow suffering in this world and condemn innocent children to eternal hell. He had read how people were screaming their rejection of God on the streets of Europe. They were leaving the churches by the thousands.

There was something else. His mother had become a warmonger. She had written him a letter describing with relish the gruesome details of the war that Napoleon III of France, Bonaparte's nephew, had declared on Prussia:

> *Luckily, we were preparing for war and could retaliate quickly. Our superior bombardment in the final siege on Paris saw the financially corrupt French officials surrender after a short six-month action. The French were forced to hand over the Provinces of Alsace and Lorraine to our victorious Kaiser, increasing the boundaries of a proud new Germany. We are now the greatest force to reckon with here in Europe.*

Yes, Karl's world was changing: his religion, his mission, his wife, his mother: everything was changing. He was confused. Life had no value or meaning for him, he could no longer cope, he knew that he needed help but he had nowhere to turn.

The tension in his body would not go away. His brain
would not rest, it would not let him sleep...

When Gudrun awoke the next morning Manduk was
gone. He had replenished the fire, leaving his hunting
spears and small dillybag so that she would know he
was far away and would return. She stretched her arms
high above her head and got to her feet. In the bright
light she examined the cave's artworks. Simultaneous-
ly, in the cold hard light of day, she reflected on
her night flight from the mission. She had no regrets,
she was swept up in the excitement of the moment.
She would invent a story for Karl. As for her future, she
had no plans.

She could see for miles from the cave opening. It
was situated high on a mountain side overlooking
Coonabarabran and the Castlereagh river. Smoke arose
from the many campfires in the valley. She spotted
Manduk as he climbed the rise carrying a large wild
duck. He looked magnificent, she thought as she
watched him carefully select his footing on the rocks,
choreographing a dance sequence that would lead him
back to the cave.

The morning was spent eating, attempting to talk
in depth and comparing their two languages. Gudrun
envied Manduk's aptitude for language. He had an ear
for it and could mimic so well. But above all else she
envied his nakedness, his openness. Suddenly, without
warning or forethought, she stood up and began to
take off her clothes. Manduk watched in fascination.
Finally she stood naked, her body enveloped by the
coolness of the fresh breeze that passed through the

cave. *Freedom*, she thought, *this is freedom.* She walked outside, sure of the fact that no European would see her and be shocked. Manduk understood; he followed her and said nothing. Gudrun continued to walk along the sandstone ledge until she reached the edge of the precipice that offered a commanding view of the whole valley. She stood perfectly still for a moment, then opened her arms, spread her legs and closed her eyes in ecstasy.

# NINETEEN

"I don't like you using money," Ginny's mother told her one day. "What happens when you run out of money and can't get any more?"

"I'll dig some yams," Ginny said, smiling.

"Will you?" her mother asked sarcastically.

"Of course … " Ginny became serious. "What is it, Mother? What's wrong?"

"The old ones are concerned that our youngsters are losing interest in the old ways and taking on the white man's ways instead," the older woman blurted out. She looked down; her face took on an expression of sadness.

"It won't happen," Ginny said.

"It is happening, even now!" Her mother became animated as she continued. "Our people rely on money more and more every day. This has happened to you — and you were raised with little knowledge of the white people. But today you speak their language as well as they do, you use their money in their shops."

"I can always get their money from selling my crafts," Ginny insisted.

"What if they stop buying?" her mother pressed on. "What if you can't get any more money? Will our daily work for food be neglected while you go begging?"

"I'll only make and sell my crafts after my daily gathering is done," Ginny promised. She gave her mother's shoulder a squeeze as she stood up and went to find her father. Ginny knew she must compromise in order to keep her mother happy. This was no time to tell her about Eugene Griffin's gentle courtship.

Some of the men were back from their hunt but Ginny couldn't see her father. Children ran and played around the huts. Ginny walked the perimeter of the camp, enjoying the atmosphere. The succulent smell of game cooking made her hungry. She found a high rock overlooking the camp and while she waited for her father's return she sat thinking about how she might fit into the new, second nation being forged by white people.

Ginny's father had hunted with the same five men all his adult life. She saw the two large kangaroos they carried into the camp on their shoulders. They were always successful, she thought.

Her father was getting old; his hair was white. When did it happen? When did he get old? Living away from her family, it seemed he had become old between visits. What would he think of Eugene Griffin? She stayed on the rock to rehearse her explanation to her family and the clan.

Andrew Tweedie hurried through Green Park carrying a satchel under his arm. The warm, clear Spring day gave notice of an early summer. He sucked air deep into his lungs as he slowed, turned into Piccadilly and went on to the hotel in Jermyn Street where he was to meet Douglas.

Douglas was already there, waiting for him. He exclaimed at his friend's appearance. Andrew's face was white and drained, his hat sat awry on his head.

"Please excuse the way I look, I've been up all night, Douglas." Yet Andrew's voice sounded triumphant. "And" — he smiled as he looked at his friend — "we've got him! Seven years ago MacInnes set up two companies in partnership with his brother: Scots Wholesale and Highland Industries. They bought produce from Wiltshire Produce and sold it back and forth between each other, running the price up. Then they finally sold it back to Wiltshire Produce at inflated prices, creating very high profits for their own companies. Scots Wholesale and Highland Industries packaged and labelled the goods differently, but they were the same goods none the less."

Douglas listened grimly as Andrew detailed how he had uncovered the complicated method MacInnes had successfully used to embezzle a fortune from his Great-Aunt. That afternoon he took Tweedie and his evidence to the chambers of Mathews, Dunlop and Fraser. He wanted MacInnes to feel the full force of British justice for his deceit and greed.

Manduk sat by the fire, pushing long straight sticks into the flames. Gudrun watched, filled with a warmness that radiated outwards. Manduk took a stick out of the flames and blew on it.

"This will make a good firestick for travelling," he said. "Tonight is the best time."

She knew he was right. They had stayed in the cave for three days and nights. Both had reached their physical and mental peaks. This was the end of an exciting episode that she would cherish for ever. It had to end. It was right to end it now. If she stayed longer there would be an unspoken agreement that she would remain Manduk's woman for ever. She opened her bag, took out her clothes and began to dress.

They spoke only intermittently on the return journey. Gudrun followed Manduk's expert footing down the hillside, but once at the bottom she clung to his arm and walked by his side. In the dark, with her vision greatly reduced, Gudrun's other senses became more acute: she discovered she could hear and smell much better as they walked slowly along the dusty road. She could hear the faintest rustling of grass as snakes and goannas retreated from them. She could smell animal droppings; the damp earth surrounding waterholes and creeks; eucalyptus trees and the exquisite sweet bouquet of wild bush flowers. Once more night veiled the lovers as they retreated to the mission to resume their lives there.

"My people never did those killings," Manduk said unexpectedly. Obviously he had been thinking about this subject for some time.

"Do you mean the homestead killings?" Gudrun asked.

"Yes. Black people don't kill like that."

"Like what?"

"Leaving things which belong to us where we kill people. You know … we are very cunning when we kill. No one knows we are coming and no one knows when we have gone. And the sticks they found near those dead people are sacred, strictly for use in ceremonies.

The spears they found are for hunting little animals. We don't use woomera for something close by, only when we are far away. And the women's things they found are for cooking."

Very slowly, the implications of Manduk's speech reached inside Gudrun's brain. Her head seemed to explode in a rush of blood. Her face reflected her revelation as she said under her breath: *"Karl is the killer!"* Her whole body shook. And suddenly she realised that she was to have been the next victim of the *Aboriginal* murderers. The artifacts strewn around her bedroom ... they had been carefully placed there by her husband! She sought desperately for his motive. Of course! The mission always increased its population each time a murdered body was found. Her brain raced as she walked on. Karl had known most of the murdered people, some of them very well. Could she possibly be wrong? In her heart Gudrun knew she was right.

"What did you say?" Manduk asked.

"Nothing," Gudrun said softly.

"We will find out who did the killing and deal with him using our own law," Manduk said. "We are not so stupid as to kill people in such a clumsy way."

Gudrun thought about what she could do with her suspicions concerning Karl. She could go to Coonabarabran to tell the police. Would they believe her? What if they did not believe her? She could confront Karl with it, face to face. — No, he was far too dangerous. If she was right he would try to kill her again ... Yet she had loved him once and he had loved her.

"It's Karl," she said, and began to cry.

Manduk looked at her. She told him about the artifacts strewn around her bedroom and why she thought Karl had killed the homesteaders. "His mission is his dream. He couldn't sit idle, he could not fail his church. They placed a huge burden on him. They had so much faith and confidence in him — he thought he had to succeed, at any cost."

Manduk became enraged.

"I can't go back to him," Gudrun said.

"I know a place you can stay," Manduk told her.

They changed direction, Manduk leading the way north through the dense scrub. They walked all night, and at noon the following day they arrived at an Aboriginal camp. Gudrun recognised a few faces — some of these families had lived on the mission at one time or another.

With Manduk's help, Gudrun constructed a gunyah a respectable distance from the other huts in the camp. That night Manduk disappeared. She knew he planned to resolve the question of Karl's guilt or innocence. She felt nervous, scared and frightened. There was nothing she could do: she just had to wait. Manduk would return soon — she had complete confidence in him. It suited her to remain at this camp for the present, a safe distance from Karl. She had not yet come to terms with the fact that he was the *Aboriginal* killer.

That night Gudrun was unable to sleep. She pulled her journal and a pencil from her carpetbag and settling herself on a blanket close to the light of the fire, she began to write.

*18th March, 1871*

*Today I have completed my fifth day of living in the bush. I am at a mountain camp near the Neuberg mission.*

*The sense of ownership (or lack of it) among Aboriginal people baffles me. I gave Ngarlu, my friend, a scarf as repayment for a favour she did for me this morning. By afternoon it was on another woman's head. She told me she had given it away. In an effort to find out about Aboriginal social ownership and responsibilities in the community, I asked Ngarlu if she would explain her custom to me. This is what she told me:*

*Certain objects are personally owned, such as a woman's digging stick, a man's favourite spears, a variety of sacred objects. Each child has to learn about the community and the duties, debts, rights and credits that adults commit themselves to throughout their lives. Mostly, these are governed by how close the borrower or lender is to you. You own kin receive special treatment. All gifts and services are reciprocal. Everything is repaid in kind or with its equivalent within a certain period. Communal ownership as such does not really exist.*

*What Ngarlu described to me is not far removed from our own European system.*

Gudrun adjusted the pencil in her hand, drew a line across the page underneath the last passage and continued:

*I have been concerned lately about Aboriginal justice...*

At this point her hand cramped around the pencil and she stopped writing. The fire glowed. Gudrun was frightened. She curled up in her blanket, wondering about her future ...

# TWENTY

"All rise!" the Bailiff called loudly. The Judge swept back into the courtroom at the Old Bailey, his red robe trailing impressively behind him as he walked in to resume his seat. He sat in the high-backed chair that carried the Royal coat of arms. It stood on an elevated platform at least five steps higher than the body of the court, where other lesser mortals were seated. The room was hushed into a prolonged silence. Finally the Judge began to speak, slowly and deliberately.

"James Henry MacInnes, the jury has found you guilty of fourteen counts of embezzlement … it is now my duty to pass sentence upon you." The large timber-panelled room reverberated with his voice. He looked directly towards the prisoner at the bar. "In the name of Her Gracious Majesty, Queen Victoria, I sentence you to be taken to the place from whence you came, namely Newgate Prison, and to be kept at that place for a period of fourteen years — one year for each of the counts found against you. You are to be employed there at hard labour at her Majesty's pleasure. With God's help you will be released a different man from the person who now stands before this court."

The Bailiff struck the bench with his gavel. "This court is now adjourned."

A collection of mumbled reactions was heard around the crowded room. James MacInnes's face turned a sickly white. His eyes had sunk back into his skull over the last few months and his greying hair had begun to fall out.

"I am innocent," he protested in a feeble voice that was barely audible. His words failed to convince even himself. His wigged barrister shook his head and pulled apologetically at MacInnes's sleeve. Two police constables seized the prisoner's arms and led him away.

Douglas sat back in his seat and folded his arms. Andrew, seated next to him, stood up. "Let's get out of here," he said: he longed to put this unhappy episode behind them.

The two men walked out into the street. It was a rainy afternoon. The traffic on the roads had come to a standstill. Coachmen screamed and yelled at the unseen carriage ahead that blocked their way. Foul air had coloured everything yellow-brown. The smell of sulphur permeated the city.

The two men talked very little as they walked away from St Paul's as far as Blackfriars Bridge, then turned west along the Thames Embankment. Hundreds of seagulls swooped and dived into the brackish water. Soon they were at Charing Cross, where Andrew hailed a cab and left Douglas to complete his journey home.

During the following months, Andrew Tweedie went to work to implement a new regime. Together with Magnusson, Douglas' other company manager, he amalgamated all Douglas' commercial produce interests into one company and all his financial investments into another. Andrew gained an enviable reputation in the City, and the profits of the Langton companies continued to increase.

It was Andrew who also contracted the services of Mortimers, the prestigious art gallery, on Douglas' behalf. They agreed to mount and travel Douglas' exhibitions, thereby greatly fostering his career in England and elsewhere. With the successful reorganisation of his business affairs and this new art gallery association, Douglas could now devote all his time to painting. Everything else was taken care of for him by others.

He decided to travel north again, to the Lake District. After an absence of many years he found that very little had changed. Once again he became absorbed in his painting. One evening at dinner, at the suggestion of a complete stranger he met in a hotel in Grasmere, he decided he would go to Scotland.

As he passed farther north, he was surprised to find how quickly the land forms changed, rising into craggy foothills along the road past Stirling Castle. Past Callander, well into the Highlands, Douglas decided to stop at Kingshouse. He was in Clan MacGregor country here. The landlord of the inn where he stayed told him the outlaw Rob Roy was buried about two miles away, in the village of Balquhidder. Douglas set out on foot the next morning to find the grave of Sir Walter Scott's hero.

There were two churches at Balquhidder, one only recently completed. The other was in ruins, beyond repair. Rob Roy's grave had pride of place, situated in front of them both on the rise from the narrow roadway. Immediately Douglas set about painting a small sketch of the scene in oils. Loch Voil reflected the red setting sun. The still waters of the small lake acted as a mirror as a heavy mist drifted up the glen.

He stayed for some weeks, painting in and around this ancient Gaelic village. His crated paintings were received with excitement at Mortimers, and an exhibition was planned for the autumn.

Douglas returned to London one day before his exhibition was to open. Harold Mortimer, the owner of the gallery, had been in an anxious state for the whole of the past week. He feared Douglas Langton would not be back in time for the extravagant opening he had planned. His anxiety was fuelled by the fact that Edward, Prince of Wales, would be present. The Prince, a well known gambler and womaniser, was the centre of London's elite social set; he was also an art lover and a generous patron of the arts.

Edward arrived at the Gallery with a large entourage. Harold Mortimer ushered Douglas forward to meet the Prince. "Sir, may I introduce you to Douglas Langton, the artist," Mortimer said in thespian-like tones.

Douglas was overwhelmed. He had not imagined he would be in awe of the Royal presence. He walked beside the Prince and in spite of his nervousness he managed to explain some of the finer points of his works. Edward was particularly interested in the painting of Rob Roy's grave at Balquhidder. He told Douglas he had attended church there the previous year. He instructed his aide to buy the picture. Douglas found it hard to concentrate on what was happening around him. The gallery was filled with people closing around the Prince and the painter as they continued their tour of the exhibition.

Afterwards, Douglas was told that the Prince of Wales had bought three of his largest works.

Following the tremendous emotional heights reached in the aftermath of his successful exhibition, Douglas fell into a deep, lonely depression. During the weeks that followed, he found he could neither work nor become interested enough in anything that would take him out of his Sussex house.

He had converted the old, Romanesque conservatory into an enormous studio. Northern light flooded through the high glass roof and three glass walls. Twenty or so unfinished works lay stacked in piles around the room. Each day he went to his studio after breakfast. He would recline on a couch, daydream, read, do anything but paint or sketch. One day, seven weeks after his exhibition, he went to the studio before breakfast. He lay back on the couch and closed his eyes. Much later he was woken from a deep sleep by Harold Mortimer. It had grown dark: the whole day was gone. Douglas was shocked. He had slept all day, he had not eaten nor spoken to a living soul; he was wasting his time away. It was then that the dark, engulfing concept of death overwhelmed him — the nothingness of eternity, the silent, unknowing blackness that awaited him at the end.

How had they learned to speak English so well, so soon, Karl asked himself as he walked past groups of blacks who sat gathered around the campfires. They're talking about me — I'm sure of it, he thought. He walked a little closer: he distinctly heard one of the men speak with a London accent.

"Look out, he's coming closer. He wants to eavesdrop on our conversation."

"Well, let him," said another. "The blighter doesn't know when he's not wanted."

Then the second man who had spoken turned and smiled at him. "We would like you not to intrude on our conversation, Pastor Maresch."

Karl couldn't believe his ears. "I'm sorry ... I'm ... I'll leave," he said, forcing a smile of his own. As he walked away he heard them continue their talk: "He's the killer, everyone knows it. It's only a matter of time before they lock him away — or better still, hang him."

At this, Karl swung round sharply. "Who said that?" he shouted. He almost ran back to the group. The men leapt to their feet and struck defensive poses as Karl went on shouting. "I want to know who said that!" His face swelled with rage; he reached out and took the nearest black man by the hair and pulled back his head. "It was you, wasn't it?"

"He can't speak like you," one of the other men said. "He only talks Kamilaroi."

Karl let the man go and broke into a run as he went back to the house. *Am I mad? Am I going insane?* he asked himself. An uncontrollable panic took hold of him. He looked about: everything was turned to a shade of grey, with a few red hues bleeding through the haze. Was he dying? He ran onto his porch and through the front door. He eased himself onto the couch and closed his eyes. *If only I could sleep. Relax*, he thought to himself, *relax*. Constant sharp pains stabbed at his eyes from inside. It was five days since Karl had last slept.

The feeling of panic eased at last. Karl dared to open his eyes. The charcoal sketch of Gudrun by Douglas Langton smiled at him from the living-room wall, her eyes penetrating his. *It's alive*, he thought. The sketch had her soul trapped in it and now it was being released. It smiled at him as if to say: We all know, Karl, you can't hide from us. He began a long conversation with the portrait. He knew it was all taking place in his mind, but he was comforted by the fact that God was allowing it to happen. *Finally*, he thought, *I am blessed with a spiritual gift*.

"Gudrun." He said aloud, "I am so glad you have come back." Suddenly his eyes brimmed with tears that spilled down his face as he stood up to greet her.

"I needed time to myself, Karl," he heard the sketch reply.

"I know you did. I sensed it," he said softly. "I can sense things much better now. God is helping me to understand. I feel ... more spiritual." Speaking in German, he continued to talk to her about his new plans for the mission. He gestured to the sketch as he outlined his grandiose scheme to build a city here, not only for all the black people in the colony but for white people as well. Everyone would share his vision of the future. He would construct a railway line linking Neuberg to Sydney. He would change the mission's name to Karlsberg — *Karl's Mountain*.

He became speechless as he watched Gudrun's spirit leave the sketch and walk out of the door. At the sound of her heels striking the boards of the porch, it was as though someone was pounding a sharp object into Karl's head, causing him to recoil with pain.

# TWENTY ONE

Ginny sat by the roadside waiting for Eugene Griffin. Early that morning she had gone with a group of women to gather yams from the flats near the new stock dam. She had worked hard, digging and cleaning twenty-seven large yams. On the way back they collected berries from the steep slope near the creek. Now she could spend most of the day with Eugene. She had saved some of the berries to share with him.

Kookaburras cackled and cawed their laughter across the wooded slope as Eugene appeared in the distance. Ginny stood up quickly, and as she waved she let out the warmest smile from her deepest secret place inside.

The sulky drew alongside. "Stop!" Ginny called.

"No!" Eugene called back.

They both began to laugh. She broke into a jog, eyeing the iron step that hung down from the cart. Suddenly she leapt for it.

"Yes!" Eugene laughed as she jumped onto the sulky. "You made it!"

She hit him on the shoulder as he cowered away in mock terror to the other side of the seat and the buggy bumped its way down the hill. Their voices and laughter echoed through the trees as they went out of sight around the bend. The wind swept the grass and the kookaburras cawed.

For five weeks they had met every Saturday at the same time. Ginny lived for their precious time together, but she knew her camp was rife with rumours.

A little later, Eugene lay flat on his back on a blanket that he spread under a large ghost-gum tree. Ginny sat upright beside him, her legs coiled. They had eaten the bread and meat Eugene had brought for their picnic lunch, and now Ginny spread her freshly picked berries on the blanket.

"I've heard about Aboriginal marriages," Eugene said suddenly. "They are arranged by the parents, aren't they?"

"All Aboriginal people are not the same. We do different things, just the same as white people."

"But tell me, do your people say who you must marry, or can you choose?"

Then Ginny saw it in his eyes. She smiled. My goodness, she thought, he wants to marry me. "I'll tell you," she said solemnly. "Some Aboriginal people have their parents arrange marriages for them. The whole clan takes the man to a secret place and the bride's sister holds his penis while his future father-in-law cuts his foreskin. Then he is allowed to marry her." She held her hand in front of her mouth, choking back laughter.

Eugene jumped to his feet. "Sweet Jesus!" Then, realising he had been taken in by her joke, he fell to the ground laughing.

"It's true," she laughed. "It's true."

Eugene rolled over, settled on one elbow and took a deep breath. He looked at Ginny, his face serious now. "Have you got a sister who will hold my penis for the cutting?"

"No … only the desert people do that, it is not the custom here." She too was serious now.

"I want you to be with me, Ginny — will you marry me?" he asked her. He took her by the hand and kissed her, and they made passionate love, their bodies entwined in the shade of the huge silvery tree.

The ride back was quiet. Ginny suggested that Eugene should come to her camp to talk with her parents and friends from the clan. Eugene was nervous, but he was prepared to agree to whatever she asked. As they drew closer to her camp, he asked many questions about Aboriginal laws and customs. He settled down once they were in sight of the smoke from the fires. She took him by the hand and they walked up to her father, who sat near his fire. He watched them as they approached. A crowd soon gathered as everyone realised what was happening. One of their own wanted to marry a white man and go to live in his world.

The elders of the Gunnedah clan had some doubts about Ginny's future with Eugene Griffin. The children could not be raised embracing Aboriginal customs; they would be light-skinned like others of mixed marriages and therefore not accepted by white people. Eugene convinced them that white men would not recognise an Aboriginal form of marriage, and he was right. It was decided that they should stay in an Aboriginal community where their children would be welcomed but marry according to the white man's custom if that was what they wanted.

Ginny told Eugene that she would feel uncomfortable living amongst her own people. She would prefer to live away from Gunnedah, at the Neuberg Mission; there it would be simpler to ease their way into their new lifestyle. They both knew it would be difficult to bridge the gap between their two peoples and cultures. But they were strengthened by their feelings for one another. They felt that together, they could do anything.

Two weeks later, Eugene Griffin and Ginny of the Kamilaroi people were married in the tiny chapel at Gunnedah. It was a simple service, modified for the predominantly Aboriginal presence in the congregation. Eugene bought Ginny a beautiful white gown for the occasion. Her dark brown skin contrasted with the soft white fabric — she looked beautiful. There was no reception afterwards: people simply adjourned to the paddock opposite the church to wish the couple well. When most of the guests had gone, Ginny's mother quietly slipped a gift into Ginny's hand: it was a stone talisman identical to the one she had made several years before for Wollumbuy. Tears ran down Ginny's cheeks as she hugged her mother and father. She took Davy up in her arms and hugged him tightly too, then lifted him onto the buggy. As the three of them rode away in Eugene's old sulky she looked back, waving, until they rounded the corner at the end of town.

The road to Coonabarabran was dusty. What was once a pristine white gown quite soon turned a pale reddish-brown. Their wedding night was spent under the incredible canopy of stars which spanned the wide southern skies. The bright constellation filled five times more of the heavens than those of the northern hemisphere: it was no wonder to Eugene that Aboriginal people used them as a focal point for so many myths and legends, and believed they were the home of the Creators of all things.

The next morning they awoke early. Ginny could not remember bird song so sweet, so melodic as that morning. The sky was a deep cobalt blue, cloudless. Ginny went over to Davy, who was asleep on the back of the buggy. He awoke with his usual smile. They packed their camping things on the sulky and were quickly on the road. As they passed a deep valley, Ginny looked down the slope at the brown murky waters of a river which ran swiftly back towards Gunnedah. There was no going back for her. She felt both excited and apprehensive as she rode with her new husband to begin a fresh, new life.

Presently Eugene pulled two travel stones from his pockets. Ginny was taken aback by the sight of them; they were not meant for women's eyes. "Where did you get those?" she asked sternly.

"Your father gave them to me," Eugene said. He smiled and handed them to his new wife.

"Only initiated men are allowed to see travel stones," she said, shunning them and averting her face. "You should be honoured," she went on. "For my father to give you such a thing is a big break from tradition. He wants to be sure we enjoy safe travel through any hostile territory."

"So you can't tell me what the engravings are on them?"

"No. Don't show them to me again. It makes me feel uncomfortable. It is only for men."

"What can happen? If you do see one, I mean."

"I can die."

Eugene looked puzzled, but he believed Ginny. It could happen. He had heard stranger things about the magic of the Aborigines.

The sun was directly above them. The heat grew intense and they decided to pull off the road and shelter in the shade. Davy fell asleep, exhausted. Eugene lay flat-out on his back in the tall grass with Ginny beside him. He had so many flies on his face that it made her laugh. He swished and swatted but these species were made of sterner stuff. No sooner had they left his skin than they flew in a semicircle and returned to exactly the same spot within a split second. She helped him control the pests with a short leafy branch that she pulled off a nearby sapling. Soon they both fell asleep.

Back on the road, *Fella*, Eugene's horse, slowed down considerably. Tired as she was, she pulled her load obediently for her master.

"How far do you think it is to the mission?" Eugene asked Ginny.

"You can see it from that rock there." She pointed to a huge sandstone boulder, miraculously balanced halfway up a steep slope.

"*Fella* is hot and tired. We have to stop again," he said.

The big horse welcomed the pull of the reins. Without any further coaxing she drew the sulky off the road, beneath the shade of a huge tree. Then she lowered her neck and started to eat the tall dry grass.

It had been dark for more than an hour when they eventually drove through the mission gates. There was less activity than Ginny remembered. Only a few glowing fires dotted the sloping landscape of the mission — those small campfires that defied the darkness and provided light for the remaining families. Ginny did not know that Manduk had visited the mission the week before, making known Gudrun's suspicions about Karl. In five days or less the Neuberg population, so painstakingly built up over two years, had fallen from one hundred and seventy souls to only thirty.

Sergeant Thompson and his men rode to Neuberg Mission next day in a deliberate line across the road, to avoid the dust created as the horses' hooves pounded into the powdery red dirt. The big Sergeant sat his horse well at a half-canter. The six men that accompanied him, three white and three black, wore masks of fearless determination. Three black trackers had arrived from Queensland to join the much talked about black muster. The desertion of Aborigines from Government missions was treated as a deadly serious matter. Aborigines from rival clans were sent in to do the job.

Karl went down to greet Sergeant Thompson and his men as they dismounted in front of the mission church. The sound of the horsemen attracted all the blacks, and the camp dogs yapped their usual welcome.

"A black has to be trained just the way you train a dog. We'll only bring back those that don't give too much trouble. The trouble-makers won't be coming back at all." As Thompson said this he caught a glimpse of a white face in the dark-skinned crowd. It was Eugene, standing beside Ginny among the mission Aborigines.

"What are you doing here?" he asked in his booming voice, walking towards Eugene.

"I have come to live here with my wife," Eugene replied, straightening to his full height.

"And who might she be?" Thompson asked, smiling sarcastically.

Eugene, using some polite sarcasm of his own, introduced his new wife. "She is right here. Mrs Griffin, meet the local Sergeant of Police. He is here to protect and defend us."

The Sergeant looked at Ginny. "Don't I know you?" he asked, frowning.

"No," Ginny replied, "you don't know me at all."

"Oh well, you know what they say," Thompson remarked, turning away. "You can't tell one black from another."

"Some people are more observant than others," Ginny retorted confidently.

The Sergeant turned back, his face suffused with blood. He was not used to being spoke to in that manner by anyone, let alone an Aborigine — and a woman at that. "You ... you just remember one thing, you're not white. You may speak our lingo and be married to a white man, but you're still black." Thompson's voice increased in volume as he spoke. He took a threatening step forward. Defiantly Eugene and Ginny stood their ground.

"The Lord above said we are all equal in His eyes, Sergeant. Do you question your God's word?" Ginny asked with a crooked smile.

The God-fearing Sergeant stopped in his tracks. He looked sideways at Karl; he knew the Abo woman was right. She had trapped him nicely in his own philosophy. He spluttered something under his breath, threw a cursory glance at the cross on top of the short church spire and turned his attention back to Karl, who had watched the scene with interest. They discussed the task at hand, how they would retrieve the blacks for Karl, and keep them on the mission.

The black people, amazed at Ginny's aggressive attitude, flocked around her offering their praise and support. No one, black or white, male or female, had ever confronted the fat Sergeant like that. Ginny displayed sharp wit and guile. She had also shown that she could use the white man's language as well as any one of the Europeans themselves. Young as she was, Ginny had already faced death; her husband and youngest child murdered by the white man. Her rape at the hands of the fat Sergeant and his cronies was very little compared to that. She feared nothing now.

# TWENTY TWO

It was late afternoon, the time of day Gudrun enjoyed most at the Koori camp. The men came back with the spoils of their hunt. The women, with fresh fires blazing, welcomed them. There was always much chatter as stories of the day were told. The children gave their own spontaneous welcome to the men.

Smoke drifted across the open space. In the distance Gudrun saw two figures walk out of the dense mulga scrub. As they drew closer, she realised one of them was white. Fear seemed to squeeze her heart. Now they were closer … she could see the white man's face. She could not believe it. Her whole body went limp. It was not Karl. It was Douglas Langton! He had a black man, a guide, with him. As he walked into the camp, he looked about anxiously. He had not seen her yet.

"Douglas!" she called.

He had found her.

He dropped the camping gear he carried and ran towards her. She barely had time to stand before he swept her up into his arms and began to kiss her, lightly at first, tender kisses. He held her head between his hands and looked long at her face. He peered deep into her eyes, then kissed her again. Gudrun wept — she felt so totally overwhelmed. She held him tightly, then buried her head in his chest and sobbed loudly.

Meanwhile, a dark, shadowy figure watched from the underbrush then slipped slowly out of view— Manduk.

Douglas knew he had made the right decision. He knew they belonged together. Not the massive oceans of the world, not anything nor anyone, would ever keep them apart again.

Word travelled quickly that a meeting had been called by the elders of the Kamilaroi in the Warrumbungle region. Black people were being forced to action by the aggressive attitude of the police. They came a few at a time at first, then as other, bigger groups arrived, the gathering grew larger. Slowly, over five days, two thousand Kamilaroi people assembled on the streets of the small township of Coonabarabran. Most white people living in the town and on its outskirts fled, fearing an uprising. Others armed themselves and locked their doors.

Many of these Kamilaroi people had not met each other before. The elders adjourned the clans to a large field where fires could be lit, corroborees performed and stories told. That was the Kamilaroi custom, to inform and entertain each other before any important discussions took place.

Sergeant Thompson and his posse received word of the gathering when they were still engaged on their muster on the other side of the mountains. They had captured thirty or more blacks and had them in irons. The police were forced to move slowly, keeping pace with their captives. The Sergeant sent one of his black trackers ahead to report news of their progress to Coonabarabran. After observing the huge Aboriginal gathering from a hilltop, the Queensland black tracker rode back at full gallop. Thompson could see the man was practically paralysed with fear. He told the Sergeant he hadn't seen so many black people in his life, that the whole town was overrun by blacks. He tore off his police uniform, hit his horse hard with the flat of his hand and rode off quickly in the opposite direction. The other two black trackers quickly followed suit. Thompson's loud yells for them to return echoed through the valley. In vain: the three white policemen were left to resolve their own dilemma.

After a few minutes' thought, Thompson gave the word to his men to let the captured blacks out of their irons, one at a time, and send them separately on their way. An hour later the three police officers rode with some trepidation towards the town.

Douglas and Gudrun had joined the Kamilaroi clans at their meeting ground. It was a spectacular sight. The group had chosen an area near a grassy knoll, enabling them to use it as an amphitheatre for the corroborees. Hundreds of fires were lit, but it was the huge bonfire behind the corroboree area which gave the performances more presence.

Ginny spied Douglas and Gudrun's white faces through the crowd, and with Eugene in tow and Davy holding her hand, made her way over to them.

They had to shout to make themselves heard above the singing that had now begun in earnest. Then they moved to a quieter spot, while Davy ran off to join a large group of other children who had discovered a waterhole nearby.

They had much to catch up on. Gudrun and Douglas listened in horror as Ginny told them how she had been a victim of the massacre at Myall Creek, her recovery, and her subsequent marriage to Eugene. Gudrun told about Douglas' return to Australia. She did not mention Karl. Douglas spoke of his long search for Gudrun. Eugene had everyone laughing about his version of how he first met Ginny.

Suddenly a hush washed over the whole assembly like a wave on a beach. Everyone in the vast crowd looked towards three uniformed figures high on the slope that overlooked the gathering. Dust flew in the air as Sergeant Thompson and his men reined their horses to a stop.

Kamilaroi warriors, eager for glory, reached for their woomeras and killing spears. A roar went up among the crowd; women grabbed their children and ran for the protective cover of the dense scrub as Thompson and his men came riding down the slope, rifles and guns held high.

Hundreds of armed Kamilaroi men ran towards the white policemen. At the foot of the rise Thompson and his men pulled their horses to an abrupt halt, threw down their weapons and, amid the rising dust, dismounted.

"I want to talk!" Thompson shouted, holding his arms straight above his head.

Black men, twenty deep, surrounded the three white men. All were nervous. From a hundred yards away Ginny came running, pushing her way through.

"They don't understand you. They can't speak English!" she shouted as she ran.

Thompson felt very much relieved to see the now familiar face of Ginny moving amongst the sea of dark heads.

"Tell them I only want to talk," Thompson told her.

"What do you want to say?" Ginny asked, regaining her breath.

At that moment Eugene broke through the circle, quickly followed by Gudrun and Douglas. They watched as Ginny translated for the Sergeant.

"He wants to end the violence!" Ginny shouted in Kamilaroi to the anxious group of black men. "He wants to meet with the elders to talk about our differences and how we can all work together."

"Tell them I don't want to hurt black people. I work for a big boss, the elder of the whole country, who tells me what to do. Tell them it is not personal." Thompson said, growing in confidence.

"I don't believe you," Ginny told him.

*"What?"* Thompson's face filled with rage.

"I don't believe you!" Ginny repeated. "I'm not going to tell them that."

Douglas and Gudrun exchanged glances with Eugene as Ginny continued: "If you want to talk about how we can live together here, without killing — that is one thing, but I refuse to tell my people anything I personally know to be false."

"Don't you … you can't … you can't give me that kind of … "

"Sergeant, I'll happily leave you to sort this mess out," Ginny said as she turned away.

"Wait!" Rivulets of sweat were running down Sergeant Thompson's face. "I'm … sorry." He struggled hard to find the right words and an acceptable tone.

Slowly Ginny walked back to the three white policemen who still had their arms high above their heads. The black men moved closer, spears poised for action. She called to the men to lower their weapons. Nothing happened. She called again, more loudly, with greater authority.

"Put down your spears!"

The spears were lowered. Ginny stood facing them. "If you wish to stop Kamilaroi blood from flowing, we have to talk with these men and talk in good faith — for now and for all the time. They represent the white elders, they are only three men, three brave men who stand alone unarmed in front of us to talk. Don't make any mistakes, they are the ones who speak for the white elders in the big cities. More white men come to the cities in their big ships every day, we won't stop them by killing these three men. It will only get worse." As Ginny continued she beckoned to the elders, who stood behind the armed black circle. "We will sit down now and talk this through. Put away your spears and nullas and let us start our talk — for our children's sake."

The group parted slowly and allowed the elders to come through. The three white men sat in the dust, immensely relieved. Ginny sat too as the black elders joined her. Several hundred young men began talking among themselves as they felt the tension easing.

Eugene heaved a huge sigh, then spoke softly to Douglas and Gudrun. "Something important is happening here." They nodded their agreement. All three were filled with emotion and relief.

Karl was determined to continue giving his Sunday sermon. The dwindling congregation numbers would not stop him. He arrived early at the church to prepare for what he knew would be a difficult day. He sat at his desk and unfolded the notes he had carefully made last evening as he sat bent over his Bible. He began writing from his notes. The ink flowed freely as line by line he laboured over the words of his sermon — words etched into his brain by the Heavenly Father Himself.

There was no movement at all in the mission grounds. An eerie quiet prevailed. A solitary bird cawed its warning to others of its kind about the unnatural quietness. The birds knew the whole area had been the home of so many people. Now there was only one.

Karl wrote beautifully; his sermon was almost complete...

The tall, dry grass sprang to life as fire spread in a neat circle around the mission grounds. It was quickly aided by the wind. The hot air that it created attracted more oxygen-filled breezes. Soon the whole area was ablaze. Deep, low, explosive sounds boomed throughout the valley as the outer mission huts ignited. Next the gardens were ablaze and the back of the school seemed to beckon the dancing flames. Karl's house was quickly engulfed as the flames found fresh fuel within.

It was unclear whether Karl heard the fire or the explosions. He continued to write: he was inspired, possessed...

The taller trees became swept up in the wind-driven fire, their dry, leafy tops instantly reduced to crisp charcoal.

Finally, Karl looked up from his notes to see the large figure of Manduk filling the frame of the church door. He stood there in full ceremonial paint, the fire he had lit raging behind him. Karl looked through the windows: he was totally surrounded by fire. He smiled at Manduk and took his place at the pulpit just as the flames licked at the dry timbers of the church.

"Today the lesson I shall read is from the Book of Proverbs... Proverbs 9:13":

*"A foolish woman is clamorous:*
*She is simple, and knoweth nothing.*
*For she sitteth at the door of her house,*
*on a seat in the high places of the city.*
*To call passengers who*
*go right on their ways:*
*Whoso is simple, let him turn in hither:*
*And as for him that wanteth understanding,*
*she saith to him,*
*Stolen water is sweet, and bread eaten*
*in secret is pleasant.*
*But he knoweth not that the dead are there; and*
*that her guests are in*
*the depths of hell."*

"And now let me draw the parallel of today's lesson for you..." Karl looked up briefly at Manduk, standing at the burning doorway. "This new country, Australia, is surely a version of the woman in the Bible who beckons us to join her as a guest. We, who are already here, know that we are certainly in hell. Make no mistake!" He gestured around himself at the burning inferno. His eyes bulged, he began to stumble over his words as he continued: "Newcomers ... most newcomers ... most newcomers lack the understanding required to live here. Live, here ... in Australia. Her land is so pure. We have eaten her bread in secret and her stolen water is ... so sweet."

Manduk raised his spear. With five strides forward he drove his decorated javelin deep into Karl's chest. There was a dull thud as it fractured his breast bone, piercing fleshy muscle to protrude six inches from his back. He stumbled awkwardly and fell backwards.

"Sweet water ... stolen land," Karl Maresch muttered at the last.

His mouth fell silent but his eyes remained open. He felt the heat of the flames as they spread from the walls across the floor beneath him. He smelled his skin roasting. He saw it slowly turn dark brown and crack open, allowing his flesh to bake. He could smell his flesh burning. He heard his hair frizzle as it singed back to his scalp...

Manduk ran quickly over the burned area that surrounded the charred mission. He wore sandals fashioned from bark, the way he'd learned from his father, so that the tough soles of his feet would not be burned. He carried a heavy load of food in his dillybag, enough for several days, and his spears and woomera. During his escape he took seldom used trails, difficult trails which required good climbing skills to scale some of the mountainous sections. As he approached the steep slopes of the Warrumbungles, he paused briefly to take off his sandals. He needed to regain the use of his toes for the narrow rock-ledge footholes of the steep Belougerie Spire.

Several hours later he lay exhausted on a flat part at the top of Belougerie Spire. He felt no remorse for killing the Lutheran Pastor. He understood the Police sergeant would pursue him for his crime, but he was confident in his ability to avoid being tracked down, confident he would not be captured. When he regained his breath and his muscles ached no more he looked along the valley, back towards Coonabarabran. He could see the smoke from the many campfires that burned at the Kamilaroi meeting grounds. He knew Ginny and the elders would find a way forward, especially now that the Coonabarabran Kamilaroi were united, and he knew Douglas and Gudrun would find their way forward, especially now.

# THE END